The Outlaw

By John And...

Barbara,
Hope you enjoy the
Story!
God Bless you!

Published by TKO, Inc
897 Via Lata Ste. K,
Colton, CA 92324

www.theoutlawpreacher.com

Printed in United States of America


ISBN # 978-0-9856412-1-4

## Acknowledgments

The author would like to thank Chris Wheeler for an outrageous book cover.   He can be reached at: cw@ignitedsgn.com

Also for the most patient and professional editor a writer could ask for: Jami Carpenter at www.redpengirl.com

May God bless you both and get ready for more *Outlaw Preacher* books coming soon!

For a schedule of the release of the next *Outlaw Preacher* book, please visit: www.theoutlawpreacher.com

Chapter One

"Man, it's cold," James uttered to himself as he braced against another biting gust. Poetic justice for the many occasions he had called friends and family back in Detroit to tell them how nice the weather was in California. The last call was three years ago and right now it might as well have been another lifetime. January in Sacramento could get your attention, especially morning and morning it most certainly was. Still dark kind of morning, his best guess was somewhere close to five, five-fifteen maybe.

He'd been walking about an hour and if not for the lights of the approaching diner he might have just hidden out under the overpass until the morning light brought a measure of warmth. But he was too close now and the thought of some hot coffee, some "real" coffee, kept his aching legs moving forward. *It's not just the cold,* he thought, *it's the freaking wind.* A very distant memory trekking across the frozen tundra, which was the campus of Michigan State University in January, triggered the thought that he had gotten soft over the years. *Fat chance*, he laughed to himself.

Maybe soft in the head but thanks to his recent situation, his physical condition was excellent. He trudged onward for another several minutes, the aches born of many poor decisions resonating through his fifty-year-old frame. He arrived at the diner and pushed the horizontal handle on the glass door, which opened faster than he anticipated and he stumbled inside.

"Good morning," came a voice from somewhere as he entered the brightly lit coffee shop.

"Good morning to you, wherever you are." James looked around as he shielded his eyes from the intrusive fluorescent light hanging just over the front door threshold. The friendly laugh suggested that the sound originated from a corner table. The voice belonged to a plus-size strikingly beautiful thirty-something waitress.

"Have a seat; you look like a deer in the headlights," she said, still laughing.

"Aren't these lights illegal in this state?" he asked with a smile.

"Probably, there ain't nothin they haven't legislated 'round here," she responded without hesitation. James liked her right away. There is nothing better than a witty waitress at zero-dark-thirty in the morning on a bitter cold day. "You want some ..." she asked.

"Yes, please," was out of his mouth before she said coffee. They both laughed at that.

"I just made the first pot of the day and you may have the honor of the first cup," she giggled.

James caught a glimpse of her name tag. "Awesome; thanks, Janice," was all he could think to say as he picked up several pages of yesterday's *Sacramento Bee* and slid into the closest booth. He smiled and began to laugh quietly as he read.

"What's so funny?" Janice asked.

"Oh, I haven't been around in a while and I still can't get over the fact that Jerry Brown is governor again. Maybe that's how Rip Van Winkle felt when he woke up, I don't know, I just think weird things."

"Did you just get out?" she asked, handing him the steaming cup.

James stared at his coffee, "Why'd you ask me that; do ex-cons get a discount?"

"Sorry," she turned away, giggling. "Sometimes I say stuff without thinking, I didn't mean anything by it."

He was a bit put off by her abruptness but quite taken with her charm and said, "What's so funny?"

Janice spun around, refilled his cup and said, "Well, maybe it's the state-issued jacket and the gray shirt or the institutional quality ink on your forearm, or maybe you just look like you might have recently spent some time at that scary old castle down the road!" They both laughed again.

"You had me with institutional quality ink! Okay, guilty as charged. Not to change the subject, but have you any food worth eating or do I just pay the cover charge for the comedy?"

"Food's actually pretty good," she said, tossing a laminated menu at his head like a Frisbee.

Janice returned a couple of minutes later after tending to new arrivals. "Decide on anything?" she asked.

"Yeah, just some scrambled eggs, English muffin, and biscuits and gravy, thank you very much. I apologize for snapping at you earlier."

"No worries, convict, I'll just poison your breakfast, but you have yourself a nice day.

"Ex-convict," replied James. "I'll have you address me in a proper manner if this is my last meal."

"Whatever." she strolled back to the kitchen to submit his order.

It had been a long time since he'd had a casual conversation with a citizen and it was refreshing. It almost made him feel like a normal person. While he waited, he enjoyed reading the newspaper and sipping hot coffee. Simple pleasures, but appreciated by a very grateful man. When the plates arrived, James found the breakfast to be amazingly good, though the rave review possibly attributed to fifteen hours without any kind of meal, not to mention three years of highly suspect fare.

His compliments were conveyed to the chef, a Mexican gentleman in his sixties who reacted with a smile and a nod of the head.

"So, where you headed; where's home?" Her voice came out of nowhere again, something to which he was becoming accustomed.

"So Cal," he replied.

"Ooohh, Hollywood," she smirked.

"Not quite," he joked.

"How you getting there? I didn't see your Mercedes in the parking lot," Janice quipped.

"Must have been stolen while I ate breakfast; this is a bad neighborhood," James deadpanned as his half-century old eyes adjusted to the growing glow of the morning light through the surprisingly clean windows.

"Want me to call the cops?" she raised her eyebrows.

"Nah, I didn't like that car anyhow," he threw out.

"What you gonna' do for money; you got a job?" she asked.

"You writin' a book?"

"Just curious."

"I don't know, maybe I'll build bikes again ... or become a televangelist; those guys seem to make a lot of money," he offered.

"Oh, please; you a preacher? I don't think even Southern California is ready for that," she laughed and walked to the latest arrivals across the room.

*Why did I tell her that?* he thought. His faith was growing stronger; while locked up, he finished Bible courses and had been licensed and ordained and had certainly considered preaching or teaching in some capacity. What God had in store for him upon his release remained a mystery but to blurt that out to a complete stranger, well ... what was that about?

His introspective wallow was interrupted by a loud voice from across the room. "Tell him to fix it!" the man's voice bellowed at Janice as she hurried back to the kitchen. James bristled at the tone of the guy's voice. It reminded him of some of the guards. Tough guys who wanted everyone to know that the world revolved around them.

"Tell him I'll fix it for him," James told Janice as she brought him his check. "What was that all about anyway?" he asked.

"Oh, that's Earl; he's a regular here," she answered.

"A regular jerk it sounds like," James retorted.

"Pastor, that's no way to talk about one of God's children," she teased.

"Yeah, maybe but he's got no right to yell at you about anything. And it's preacher, not pastor," he offered with a grin. "I don't have the patience to be a pastor. All those people whining and complaining about the same problems day after day. Sounds more like a babysitter; no thanks!" James answered in a rehearsed diatribe.

He had formulated some semblance of a philosophy surrounding this and many other topics. Five months into his sentence James had a run-in with some inmates who had taken issue with James' refusal to 'clique up' in an official capacity. Fellow Caucasians saw fit to beat him into the infirmary, but not without significant casualties absorbed by all involved. Two of his attackers joined him, albeit requiring a shorter stay. For his participation, James received three broken ribs, a bruised kidney, and a broken nose. The broken nose was arguably an improvement as it seemed to straighten a previous adjustment he'd received courtesy of some bikers in San Bernardino years back.

Three weeks in bed and bandages allowed for some introspection and philosophizing. A chaplain's visit during his recovery sparked a philosophical debate, which led to several subsequent visits and a thorough thrashing of the prisoner's firmly held — but substantially flawed — convictions. His subsequent commitment to the Lord was facilitated by a man whose slight physical stature and soft voice should have been crushed and silenced by the rage and violence in that place. Seemingly oblivious to the degree of hate coursing through these walls, this little man moved with a quiet confidence and courage that intrigued and impressed James, who had reached a point in his life where coincidence could no longer explain his continued existence. In spite of his best efforts to ignore the calling in his life, there was still a nagging deep in his spirit against which his rage could not prevail.

*I have nowhere to go but I'm sure in a hurry to get there*, thought James. His whole life was like that, at least before his three-year forced compliance. *What a waste*. Then again, the scripture says, 'All things work to the good for those who love God and are called according to His purposes,' and he was determined to let God lead no matter how many times he released his grip.

Had James testified against those guys back then the penalty would have been far greater than three years. At least now the debt to society is paid. Technically not his debt, but someone had to pay it. James made his decision and in the process became a legend in a world to which he owed no allegiance, a dark underpinning of society of which most people have no knowledge or appreciation. Wrong place, wrong time, but then again 'all things work to the good.'

James remembered a prison chaplain who laughingly explained that the scripture did not mean all things *were* good, only that they worked out to the good. Important distinction, that! One could take a grim view of things with the wrong interpretation. False promises beget false faith or something like that. God was faithful, this much James was learning.

"Hello, earth to convict," Janice's voice pierced his daydream. "I don't even know your name," she continued.

"Huh, oh, my bad; name's James," as he reached his tattooed arm toward her firm but gentle grip. She held his hand for maybe three seconds but a female touch felt good.

"Did that hurt much?" she asked, examining his scarred up hand.

"Ha, you should see the other guys!" James shot back and changed the subject, asking about a nearby truck stop. Janice explained that the West Sacramento Truck stop was just up the highway and then excused herself to handle the increase in morning business. After calculating his current net worth at five-hundred sixty-seven dollars, James tossed a twenty down on his

$12.80 breakfast invoice, gathered his coat and black knit beanie.

"Hey wait," she yelled and walked briskly toward a startled James. "I got you a ride to the truck stop. That guy over there is a parts runner for the Kenworth dealer and he said he would take you if you need a lift."

"Well, since my 'Benz is missing, I'll take you up on that, thank you very much."

She smiled and wrapped her pale arms around his muscular frame and squeezed hard. "Take care of yourself there, Outlaw … Outlaw Preacher!" She chuckled. "It's got a ring to it. James, the Outlaw Preacher; who was that masked man?" she continued to tease him.

"Alright there, Janice, way too much fun for first thing in the morning, but thanks for your kindness and may God bless you," he said as he moved toward the door. James motioned to his ride that he'd be outside whenever he was ready. This time the morning air was invigorating and fresh, the kind of air you can taste. Northern California could produce some good air, he thought to himself. Although it was the same air a few miles down the road, free air tasted a whole lot better than state air.

"Dear Lord in heaven, thank you for this day, this new life and thank you for your son Jesus Christ," James uttered, barely audible, as he sat on a boulder with a great flat spot and a little vertical cut that fit the small of his back perfectly. He thanked God for the rock, too.

Chapter Two

The ride to the truck stop was uneventful once the men exhausted the obligatory, "Where you from," and "Where you headed," and "It sure is cold this morning," niceties. It couldn't really be called a conversation; men don't really have conversations. They mumble one-word questions and answers. A most economical if not enlightened method of communication. Studies show that women use twenty-five thousand words per day in conversation while men are a distant second with ten thousand.

James said "Thanks for the lift," and the driver nodded and said, "No problem," but did suggest that James, "have a nice day," which is about as useless a saying as "I'll pray for you," if there was never an intent to do so. James had just served three years for a crime he didn't commit, but "have a nice day," would make everything just fine!

James thought, *This freedom thing will be short-lived if I keep projecting this brand of hostility into a simple non-conversation.* Did he really just think all of that at seven in the morning? He'd gotten used to looking over his shoulder the past ten years or so both in prison and as an outlaw biker. It might take a minute to accept that he was actually free. This felt strangely reminiscent of his release from rehab twenty years ago when he, quoting from the brochure, had his whole 'new' life in front of him but after twenty minutes outside the safety of confinement, terror struck! Thoughts of *I'll never make it* came flooding at him straight from the pit of hell. In the middle of the attack it was difficult to recognize the origin of those desperate thoughts. They seemed remarkably accurate but that is just how the enemy the devil operates. He's been at this a lot longer than we have; read the book of Job sometime.

"Lord, I thank you that I am free to think and plan and live again but I can't, nor do I want to do this without your hand upon everything. Please lead me, guide me and give me ministry, let your will be done, amen." James let out an audible, if anyone was there to hear it, sigh. *If a tree falls deep within a forest with nobody there, does it make a sound?* James laughed out loud and thought, *This is no time for an acid flashback,* and headed in the direction of a trucker who was yelling at a late 90s Freightliner with its hood up.

The owner of the truck was a giant of a man with a matching voice and nothing that projected from his mouth at this moment was pleasant. James thought, *He ain't havin' a nice day,* and laughed to himself as he walked toward the man. "What's the problem, brother?" asked James.

"I ain't got no brother and if I did he wouldn't be a tore up piece of biker trash like you," barked the giant.

James shrugged, resisting the urge to crush the big man's throat and said, "Sorry I asked."

"Yeah, well this thing has cost me twice what I paid for it in repairs and right now I'm running late for a customer who don't care much about my problems. Sorry I jumped on you; I've just had enough already today," he said with his hand to his forehead.

James stuck out his arm and said, "Name's James," to which the giant said, 'Gary.' "So what's it doin', or should I say not doin'? These Detroits are great most of the time," James asked.

"It ain't buildin' air and without air, I ain't goin' nowhere," replied Gary as he lit a Swisher Sweet cigar.

James made a mental note to buy a good cigar sometime soon. "So, where you heading?" asked James.

"South," Gary replied. "Just east of Pomona."

"Well, if I can get this to build air, would you drop me off down there?" James asked.

Gary, laughing and coughing smoke said, "Sure, pal, sure thing. I'm gonna call a mobile guy and he's gonna bend me over for four or five hundred bucks or worse to replace the governor or the compressor and this stinking load's only payin' six hundred and fifty bucks so sure, knock yourself out. I'm going inside to get a coffee."

James responded, "Me, too; I'll need a big coffee to fix this thing."

"You'll need more than that," Gary mumbled.

"Lord, this is one of those times. Please let this work," James prayed as he walked to the counter with the biggest coffee the aging truck stop offered.

"We've got fresher coffee coming up in about a minute if you care to wait," the woman behind the counter suggested.

Glancing at the crooked plastic handwritten name tag, he answered, "No thanks, Maria, this will work."

"Have a blessed day," she added, handing James change from a five.

"I plan on it, Maria. God bless you, too," he answered. It's always nice to exchange pleasantries with another believer. Some Christians pepper their conversations with words like 'blessing' and 'prayer' as verbal trial balloons. Other Christians jump on those words like storm shelters in a tornado. It's code for 'we're in this together,' and it's comforting. Nonbelievers just ignore them completely, which gives them away every time. A true evangelist will forge ahead in the face of such adversity, but a closet Christian will take it as a signal to retreat. James inwardly rejoiced as his mind was returning! What a nice bonus on a sunny morning.

James headed out the door to the waiting rig. Gary was already at the truck without his coffee, which prompted James to ask him if he'd changed his mind.

"Yeah, I can't wait around drinking coffee. Either you can get this to build air, which I gotta' see to believe, or I hafta' call a mobile guy. I got some numbers from the tire shop over there." He nodded toward an open structure with a metal roof filled with old and new tires stacked head high for a good twenty rows.

"Okay, big strapper, start this thing up and let's see if we can get some air flowing," James instructed.

Gary lumbered his way up and into the driver's seat like he was climbing a rock wall. James felt for the guy. It's a hard life and when it's your truck every day is like Russian roulette with disastrous possibilities. Breakdowns, accidents, lousy drivers, inclement weather, blown tires, nasty shippers and receivers, and the constant race against an impossible schedule and like Gary said, a nine hundred dollar repair and there goes the week!

"Hey," Gary yelled over the roar of the engine. "You ain't got any tools. Is this some kinda' joke, dude, cause I ain't laughin' and the air gauge ain't moving."

"Hang on just a second," yelled James. "Well, Lord, here we go," he said out loud as he began slowly pouring the hot coffee over the missile-shaped air governor above the starter.

"What the heck are you doing?" Gary stuck his head out of the window to observe how this vagrant with no tools was "fixing" his truck. "That does it; I'm kicking your butt!" and he started out of the truck.

James yelled, "Look at the air gauge first; is it moving?"

"No, it ain't ... wait ... well, I'll be switched; it's building air!" howled Gary. "How the ... what the heck did you do you freak, you poured coffee on ..."

"The air governor cylinder expands under the heat of the liquid and the plunger releases and voila, you have air," James beamed. "Thank you, Jesus!" he yelled.

"Yeah, sure I'll thank Jesus, whatever, I'm just ... wow; it's working and the air is building all the way up."

"Let's do this then." James moved to the front of the truck and began to lower the hood. Gary met him at the driver side step and shook his hand as James finished securing the hood's rubber side latch.

"Guess I owe you a ride south, biker boy; you ready to roll?" asked Gary, mood noticeably improved.

James' outward appearance—messy shoulder length hair and graying beard topping a tattooed muscular frame — disguised his intelligent nature. Able to move from a locker room to a bar room to a board room and assimilate immediately into each, he knew something about everything but not everything about anything. Mesmerizing green eyes compensated for the surgically repaired nose, which James was almost convinced added character. After all, like his mother used to say, it would be unfair if he had all that charm, intelligence, *and* good looks!

"Let's go!" James answered as he walked around and hopped up into the passenger's seat.

Chapter Three

What Gary lacked in grace on the ground he more than compensated for behind the wheel. His thirty-year skill set was evidenced by his effortless coaxing of the tractor trailer onto Highway 80. His courage and skill needed to negotiate almost seventy linear feet of rolling iron down the highway was breathtaking. It occurred to James that truckers are the unsung heroes of the world's supply chain, especially when their eighty thousand pound missiles are making their way through an Atlanta or Houston or Los Angeles freeway system. Why these things aren't wrapped around ten thousand SUVs a day is one of the wonders of the world. The fact that most people should not be on the roads is never more evident than when sitting in a big rig in heavy traffic.

"Man, people are crazy," James said as two idiots in a tweaked-out Honda civic snaked around the truck at over eighty miles per hour, only to display their brake lights moments later.

"Uh huh, and if they live they'll be there twenty minutes before we are. I hope it makes a difference,"

Gary offered. James reflected on how this was the same guy who wanted to kill him an hour ago.

Once settled into his executive office behind the wheel, Gary became the CEO of his little empire. He fired off instructions via blue tooth to his bookkeeping and permit service and directed his insurance company to "get busy" faxing an updated certificate to a broker's home office in Modesto. Gary was in the groove now and strangely peaceful. He looked like a rock and roll drummer with all of his equipment at arm's length. Drummers can play blindfolded if the equipment is at the right height, angle and distance from the stool. Gary had his seat just right, the mirrors were perfect, CB radio microphone on a makeshift bungee cord hanging from the headliner just above his right hand. All he needed was a high hat cymbal and he could join the band.

"Hey man, how'd you know to pour that coffee? That was pretty cool. I was ready to bust you up and then ..." Gary laughed and broke the silence.

"I wondered if you were gonna ask me that or just go on thinking I was a genius," smiled James.

"Oh, I didn't think that for a minute," Gary joked with a friendly laugh.

James replied, "I knew a guy in Tulare — a mechanic — though that term doesn't do this guy any justice. Dude could diagnose stuff over the phone. Craziest thing you've ever seen. I had a couple of trucks a few years back, '96 Freightliners like this one, same kind of engines so I was somewhat familiar. I can do alternators, u-joints, water pumps, and of course, coffee tricks!" That got a laugh. "The truck whisperer," he added. They laughed again.

"Why'd you get out of trucking?" asked Gary.

"Aw, it's complicated."

"It usually is," Gary answered with an understanding tone. "Forget I asked."

James wadded up his duffel bag against the surprisingly cold passenger's window and leaned his head against it. "You can turn up the music if you want," he said, and they drove on with the sound of southern rock and the steady roar of the diesel engine. The vibration of the window against his head must have induced an alpha state in James because he was out like a light. They drove on about forty-five minutes before the potholes on the southbound 5 freeway proved too much for his attempt at a decent nap. After several direct hits to the passenger side suspension, and rather than face repeated blunt force trauma to the right side of his head, he reluctantly straightened in his seat.

James thought about the statewide budget deficit newspaper story he'd briefly entertained at breakfast and quickly deduced that no highway repairs would be undertaken any time soon. He thought about the second law of thermodynamics and how nothing stays the same and everything moves toward decay and that the 5 freeway was concrete (pun intended) evidence of that. *You think too much*, he said to himself. *About nothing*, he added, and smiled. A quick glance at his captain indicated that Gary had not moved an inch nor changed expression since his last check over an hour ago.

"How you doin'?" James asked.

"Fine as wine, we're making good time so far." he replied. "'Bout six hours to go, give or take."

James thought how another six hours of driving would appeal to the average person but how Gary just dismissed it like a trip to the neighborhood Seven Eleven. "I called the warehouse while you were getting your much-needed beauty sleep. They'll stay open for us so we can deliver this today. Guess they need this product for production."

"Cool," James answered. He hadn't given much thought to when they would arrive or what his plan would be after he got to Southern California. You'd think that with three years to plan his life he would have this dialed in but such was not the case. James had made a decision to rely on God and to avail himself to the will of God and just let things unfold in a different manner than the frantic planning which goes into most people's lives. Not total abandon; nobody has that much faith! *There should be some direction*, he thought.

The initial "plan" was to find the parking structure in San Bernardino where his motorcycle was stored, and then most likely, it would involve a visit to the bank where his sister Diane had set up his account and seeded it with the seventeen thousand eight hundred dollars that remained from his portion of their mother's estate. Diane wasn't a big fan, as his story didn't work well with her financial planner husband, their circle of friends, and the life she strived to maintain. James didn't care much; the last thing he would ever do was force a relationship. He appreciated the fact that she took the time to set up his account and he left it at that.

He figured he'd deposit much of the cash he was holding and look for a small and inexpensive storefront/warehouse in the Inland Empire. The IE was a vast territory of flophouses, bars, pawnshops, street churches, malls, fast food, fine dining, apartments, communities, and mansions. The place had it all and it could change dramatically from one block to the next. The elegant foothill region of Claremont was two miles from Pomona but might as well be a separate world, such was the contrast. Every ethnicity was represented. Crime and addiction was everywhere from the missions to the mansions. The only variables were the quality of cars, clothes, crimes, and the choices of addiction. It was the perfect place to start.

The weather in Southern California is arguably the best in the world. It's almost ridiculous with eighty degree Januarys and oil painting sunsets from any number of breathtaking mountain and shoreline vistas. Regional climatic variances allow an enterprising individual the opportunity to surf in the morning and snowboard in the evening by merely driving a couple of hours. It's an intoxicating locale to be sure.

Yet, the entire state was careening toward the cliff and doomed to a catastrophic landing without a philosophical or spiritual awakening. A spiritual awakening, or what James' earthly father would term, a 'come to Jesus' meeting, was surely needed.

Inside the prison walls, James had an epiphany of sorts. It was evident that his plans and methods were abysmally inadequate. In a moment of clarity, he had arrived at a level of awareness that 'his best thinking had got him there,' and that to trust God as entirely as possible meant casting off earthly attire. The pursuit of such an endeavor necessarily exposes the degree of expanding or diminishing trust in one's God or world view.

At some point in our individual and collective sojourns through life we all arrive at this realization. Some do willingly, some do it in prison, some on their death beds, but we all get there. We spend our lives under the delusion that we have control, yet we live in a constant state of panic reaction to life. Seriously, if we control everything, should we not examine our current station and ask ourselves, "Is this the best we can do?" Such introspection and self analysis will, if treated with integrity, drive us to our knees. If not to God, then to despair for the viability of our world view is laid bare.

*Jeez*, he thought, *My mind is a scary place*.

It must be the coffee. His mind continued with an uncharted foray into the subject of racism, learning quickly that prison is the most racist environment ever foisted on humankind. James had resisted all recruitment efforts into any of the white only gangs inside, preferring to do his time in the most anonymous manner possible under the circumstances. He remained segregated as this was a necessity for survival, but beyond hanging with 'his kind' at meal time and most certainly yard time, the rest was of little interest. It cost him some stitches and some bruises and, of course, the broken bones and re-adjusted beak, but after all was said and done he was left basically to himself, especially after word got out that he was a Jesus freak and began preaching to all who would listen and some who would not. He took the call to 'tell people about me,' very seriously.

James understood that there are only two types of people in the world, lost and saved, or as he called them, the 'lost and found.' This allowed him to remain impervious to racism, as it is not a logical position. A non-sequitur, as his philosophy professor routinely reminded him thirty years earlier. Latin for, 'it does not follow.' If you subscribe to lost and found, then color has no basis and is nothing other than a distraction and a tool for politicians to divide and conquer. Not to mention a substantial implement to be employed by the devil himself as a constant source of societal conflict. When your goal is to confuse and animate a society's members in an effort to distance them from any serious spiritual ascension and maturity, any excuse is good enough. Racial animosity is repackaged and resold to each generation, yielding ever larger dividends to the master antagonist. Keep the populace enraged and violent and they will never rise high enough above the battleground to be astounded by the circle in which they've been traveling for decades!

James' mind wandered further to the story of Moses leading his people to the Promised Land, which should have been something like a two-week trip but due to their pettiness, infighting, and cyclical insanity, some forty years elapsed with none of them ever making it to the Land of Promise. It was madness. We are all mad. *You certainly are*, he thought.

He feared his head would explode if he didn't get out of the truck pretty soon. How did a guy like him not go completely insane in prison? He regularly wondered how it would be outside those walls. The fear was upon him again and he was fighting internally with scripture that commands us not to fear and 'to be anxious for nothing' and sometimes it was so terrifyingly overwhelming that he wanted to scream and run but he had resolved to stop running.

Wasn't he running right now? Isn't there a disconnect from reality during any relocation or road trip with no accountability except to the journey? Isn't that why people run, stop, and then run some more? The constant planning, packing, driving, and unpacking excuses us from dealing with everyday problems. *Is this spiritual warfare or what? Does this ever end?* Then there is the question of degree. To what degree is spiritual warfare the prevailing assault on a believer and how much can be attributed to the worldly adage, 'life sucks, then you die?'

*Wow, you are a deeply philosophical bag of wind, aren't you?* James shook his head. He focused on the cracked lens of the digital clock that was velcro'd onto the dash of the rig, one of those small black rectangular things you can buy at a dollar store. It was nearing two p.m. One forty-seven to be exact, as if the word exact and that cheap clock could exist in the same sentence. "That clock right?" James asked.

"Oh yeah, it's synchronized with the U.S. Naval Observatory master clock," Gary laughed. "I calibrate it twice a day, Greenwich mean time minus eight."

James just looked at him and shook his head. *Ask a stupid question*, he thought. James liked Gary. A cantankerous old grouch straight out of central casting, but he was a sharp guy. Not book smart but 'this ain't my first rodeo,' kind of smart. James liked that in people. He also liked that he could impart a neat coffee trick that would no doubt be replayed at truck stops all over the west coast for years to come with absolutely no credit paid to him. James smiled. "Figure what, maybe another couple of hours?" he asked, changing the subject slightly.

"'Bout that," replied Gary, "You in a hurry?"

"Yeah, that's why I picked a broken down truck to get me from Sacramento to Pomona," which had them both laughing.

"Well, we might lose a minute or twenty 'cause I'm stopping at Frazier Park for fuel at the Flying J," added Gary.

"There goes my schedule," quipped James, who was actually relieved to be stopping. He could use a stretch and a visit to the men's room. There was only so much bouncing around he could take after the morning's coffee.

He also wanted to investigate the latest in prepaid cell phone technology, since James had no delusions about AT&T or Verizon soliciting his business, at least not right away. He'd read about it in a magazine in the prison library and made a mental note to look into it. This would allow him to begin his long journey toward citizenry. Not technically — of course he was a citizen — but in the 'I have a phone number,' sense. He had a vague plan, which included a small apartment or room somewhere, and a phone number.

James felt the truck slowing as they leveled off near the Frazier Park exit. This was one of James' favorite gas stops back when he would ride his Harley up to Bakersfield and then over to the coast on weekends or on club business. He had always liked the weather up here. It was always twenty degrees cooler at this elevation than in the L.A. basin, which could be thirty degrees less than Bakersfield, which could be a hellish place to ride in the summer. Frazier Park could be snowed in one day and sixty degrees and sunny the next, part of the romance of the place. It was also a boneyard for big rigs. The 'Grapevine,' as it's known by most who travel, is an almost forty-mile stretch of gently winding and steep grades on either side of Frazier Park and if something is going to break on these trucks it invariably happens through here. It can get scary, and expensive.

Gary jockeyed for position among the dozens of rigs pulling in and out of the Flying J Truck stop. He settled in behind a Promised Land Express Truck that was just topping off his tanks along with his refrigerated unit, so they wouldn't have too long to wait. Gary explained that a simple fuel stop could stretch into forty-five minutes if you got behind the wrong trucks. There are as many different personalities on the road as there are trucks. Some guys are in and out of a fuel stop like a NASCAR driver and others seem to want to talk to anyone who will listen. Every driver has a thousand stories and they grow longer on down the line. Sewing circles could learn a few things about gossip from these guys. It's an amazing network. James had always thought that if he could organize independent truckers he could be the wealthiest, most powerful man in America. The trick is the communication, and with the strides in technology, that day could arrive. Alas, he thought, that, too, would have to wait.

How could one guy have this much energy for enterprise but at the age of fifty have nothing thus far to show? *Knock it off*, he told himself. *It's only halftime and you're tied in a game they gave you no chance of winning. God is in control, remember?* Anything can and most likely will happen. You just have to keep at it. Perseverance alone is omnipotent. He'd read that somewhere ... Calvin Coolidge said it but it was later attributed to Ray Kroc of McDonald's fame:

*Nothing in the world can take the place of persistence. Talent will not; nothing is more common than unsuccessful men with talent. Genius will not; unrewarded genius is almost a proverb. Education will not; the world is full of educated derelicts. Persistence and determination alone are omnipotent.*

The slogan, 'press on' has solved, and always will solve the problems of the human race. James believed this philosophy even in the darkest loneliest days in Folsom prison and now he had the opportunity to prove these words true.

Proverbs 24:16 says, 'For a righteous man falls seven times, and rises again.' This must be the one trait that separates great from average. James was growing in grace and had begun his journey to the mastery of the greatest human accomplishment, trusting God. The biggest demon plaguing him was regret. There were too many times lately when he tortured himself with the 'what ifs' and the coulda-woulda-shoulda confusion that confound a person. This must be defeated as soon as it enters your head, but it has to be recognized and identified before you can defeat it. The devil can have you cosigning that nonsense before you know it. Tricky business, this spiritual warfare.

"You want anything from in there?" James asked as he pointed to the store.

"I'll take the biggest Pepsi they got," Gary answered.

James marveled at how this guy, a very big guy at that, could function on Little Debbie chocolate peanut butter bars and Pepsi because so far that's all he'd seen the man eat. James was no nutritionist but he tried, when he wasn't behind bars, to drink only water or iced tea or black coffee and eat as much raw or minimally processed food as possible. An occasional Double-Double at In-N-Out was acceptable; in fact, he had already planned to visit the one on Indian Hill Boulevard in Pomona for dinner. He did hit the gym regularly and attempt to eat decent food, but a man has to live a little. Conversely, Gary was a marvelous example of complete disregard for health. He smoked cigars, ate chocolate peanut butter wafers, and drank nothing but Pepsi, and it showed! A quick survey of the patrons of the truck stop indicated that this was epidemic in nature. The junk food purveyors were making a killing, literally.

James made his way to the technical section of the trucker store, looking like a tourist in a foreign land. There were headsets from the size of a pack of matches up to NASCAR headsets by Motorola for a hundred bucks. These weren't even the phones! When he went to prison, flip phones were the big deal and now the phones looked like video games. This was a truck stop, for crying out loud; he could only imagine what a Radio Shack must look like now. It was fascinating but all he wanted was a darn phone. He was able to flag down an employee and asked about the possibility of a prepaid phone. He was given two choices and grabbed the first one he saw: $39.95 loaded with one thousand minutes. He could add minutes when he needed them. James could not imagine anyone talking for a thousand minutes a month but he took what they suggested. He had a phone number and that was an accomplishment. The clerk told him he'd be able to purchase the phone at the register when he had finished his shopping. *Shopping?* James thought. *This is a Flying J bro, not Macy's.* He grabbed a bag of trail mix and filled what seemed like a gallon of Pepsi into the BIG THIRST plastic cup and made his way to the cashier; he had 'finished his shopping.'

As he walked outside Gary was slowly making his way toward the store, his labored gait even more noticeable than earlier in the day. James wondered how old the trucker was and what his health and life would be like without the self-induced abuse. His mind wandered to the untold thousands of other men and women in this industry who were just going through the motions, dying a slow death of poor health and bankrupt ideologies. One does not have to be on the road too long to hear the hopelessness in their voices. When the most popular answer to "How's it going?" is "Same stuff, different day," defeat cannot be too far behind. Poverty of spirit, he thought.

"I got your Pepsi," James said before Gary looked up to see him heading his way.

"Yeah, thanks; just put it in the tractor. I'll be out in a minute."

"I got a phone," James said for some unknown reason.

"Congratulations; give me the number and I'll write it on the wall in there," Gary grinned.

"I'm good," James said as he continued toward the truck. His immediate plan was to read the brochure about the phone and determine how the minutes worked. He was quite enamored by the prospect of a phone with no contracts. The less paperwork in his life the happier he was. He was a wary man and prison life did little to alter that. James believed in honor and integrity. A man's word should suffice. He knew the world did not reflect his values but he was uninterested in compromising his methods of operation. He knew the truth had to be unwavering in order to function as truth. James not only loved God, he respected Him. God was constant and holy and James was becoming quite comfortable in that knowledge.

Chapter Four

Through the bug-splattered windshield James watched Gary ambling slowly toward the rig. He was carrying a paper bag rolled up at the top. James figured it was more Little Debbie wafers. He smiled and slowly shook his head. Then he jumped from the truck and grabbed the long-handled window squeegee and cleaned the big man's windows before he arrived.

Gary was surprised by the gesture. "Thanks, Easy Money; worried I couldn't see?"

"Yeah, well, it's the only thing I'm gonna clean, so enjoy it," James laughed.

"You ready to roll?" Gary asked.

"You're in charge, driver." Both men were invigorated from the break and ready to make the final two and-a-half-hour push to the delivery point.

"Mind if I charge my phone?" James asked.

"Be my guest," Gary replied, pointing to the cigarette lighter socket. Gary ran through the first eight gears in effortless succession and after about a mile

Interstate 5 freeway leveled off to where the last two gears could be employed.

They had made the fourteen-mile climb and were now on the several-mile flat portion of the highway that would become a hair-raising 6 percent downgrade where many an inexperienced trucker has lost control, resulting in mayhem. Countless people have died over the years running the Grapevine. Passenger cars and big rigs, motorcycles and motor homes have all been claimed by this monster of a hill. The Grapevine plays no favorites and is an equal-opportunity thrill ride. The irony is that it bottoms out at the Magic Mountain amusement park. The southbound down grade is the most insidious as it lulls you with its gradual pull and then you see a warning sign that says 6 percent grade! James likened it to snow skiing where you can be cruising along enjoying an invigorating run and all of a sudden the Black Diamond Expert sign looms ahead and you can't turn around because you're already picking up speed and heading downhill. You either sit and slide and cry or ski it. Such was the ride to Santa Clarita from Frazier Park. *Have a nice day indeed!*

James was thankful that his captain was a seasoned veteran; according to Gary, he makes this trip every day Monday through Friday, twelve months a year. James figured he'd sit back and enjoy the ride as much as anyone could. This is where slow and steady wins the race.

Gary kept the rig in the far right lane and crawled down the grade, allowing the dat-dat-dat of the engine's 'Jake' brake to slow the eighteen wheeler, thus minimizing the use of the tractor and trailer brakes. There's nothing like the metallic smell of a hundred pounds of brake shoes incinerated by a frantic trucker. Gary joked that he should open a tire and brake shop at the bottom of the hill. James suggested he include a shower and laundry, which Gary found extremely funny. "Wash the fear off of you," he said. It's always funny when it's someone else.

~

Southern California! At last James had officially negotiated the gauntlet which had oppressed him for most of the trip. It was that feeling that he was never really free and the urge to glance over his shoulder was relentless. It was sad that Northern California's surreal beauty would always remind him of fear and dread and confinement. Maybe someday it would diminish and he could remember the great times riding up there but right now he knew he was being sent to Southern California and he was happy to be there. James could be dropped here blindfolded and recognize Southern California just by the incessant traffic noise. For those who have never had the pleasure of the combination of NASCAR and the 'Twenty-four hours of Le Mans,' which is the daily commute anywhere in Southern California, it is something to behold. Where else would otherwise intelligent humans voluntarily donate up to three hours each way on a violent and unforgiving cluster of freeways just to spend another eight hours in a cubicle surrounded by people who would crawl over you for another dollar an hour.

It is not unusual for a person to labor eight hours at a job and five hours driving to and from. James had priors for that behavior and was determined not to put himself in that position again. A man's life must be more than the commute where talk radio personalities become intimate friends and thoughts and passions are controlled by news, weather, and sports. It's insanity and it's voluntary. The blank or angry faces of thousands of clones pushing their way in a hopeless race against the clock and each other were everywhere. Man's inhumanity to man!

James shook the latest philosophical rant from his mind. *You need your meds*, he laughed to himself. This mental departure was not unusual; he was accustomed to these sojourns. He had always felt sorry for anyone who dared to share intimacy, as his constant mental meltdowns were worthy adversaries to normal conversation. The GPS voice, announcing the approaching destination in 'point two miles on the right,' jarred him back to reality, today's reality. They were going to a tortilla plant of all places.

Gary's load consisted of raw materials necessary for ongoing production. It seemed that the west coast had an insatiable appetite for tortillas. Gary downshifted once again as they reached the guard shack surrounded by freshly painted bright yellow vertical concrete protection posts. The age of the facility and the condition of the guard shack suggested this wasn't the first fresh coat of paint these things had seen. Gary presented the bills of lading to the guard and waited while he walked around the truck, checking the door seal for compromise. The guard conversed with someone over the hand-held radio and awarded Gary door #3 when he returned the delivery documents. Gary grumbled his appreciation and pushed the gear shift forward and released the clutch. He guided the huge rig around an alley that led to the unloading dock. "Figures," Gary spat. "These idiots stuck us in door three between two other trucks and there are seven other doors wide open."

"Lazy *and* stupid," James muttered. "Great combination." Gary nailed the backing and James could tell he enjoyed the success. It was a tight spot but the big guy just wheeled the rig using his mirrors and steering wheel for the thousandth time. James noticed the other drivers up on the dock watching Gary's work. James quickly jotted his new phone number on an old Detroit Diesel business card and placed it in the empty cup holder on his side. "You gonna need help unloading?" James offered.

"No way; they will unload it or they can pay an unloading service, 'cause I ain't touchin' it. It's all pallets and should roll right off, but thanks for the offer."

"No problem. I'm gonna get going; thanks for the ride. I left my number in the cup holder; hit me up sometime." He reached across the cab and shook the big trucker's hand.

"Appreciate the coffee trick. You take care now, biker boy."

James gathered his backpack and jacket, took a quick glance at the digital clock, which indicated 4:53 p.m., and climbed out of the truck. He had a couple of miles to walk to get to Indian Hill Avenue. He figured thirty minutes and he'd be enjoying a Double-Double at the In-N-Out burger, which was a small but quite attainable goal. He took some satisfaction in making the four hundred mile trip for the cost of a phone and a couple of dollars in Pepsi and coffee but he was feeling hunger pangs and that burger would taste great. The weather was warmer down here during the day. He could see the wind picking up by movement at the tops of the palm trees and figured "Santa Ana's" were beginning, which meant at least a few days of above average temperatures and decent nights. James was already thinking of saving the fifty bucks he'd budgeted for the night's motel, depending on the weather. He had a sleeping bag on his bike but that was a good twenty miles away. *Burger first*, he thought, and headed east.

Chapter Five

This walk was decidedly more enjoyable than the one twelve hours earlier as it represented progress. The first step of the journey of freedom had been lonely and cold, but now after four hundred miles and arriving at his destination in warmer conditions and an impending Double-Double, things were looking up. James figured another ten minutes or so and he'd arrive at the old familiar red and white sign with the yellow arrow indicating in his humble opinion the best darn cheeseburgers on the planet. He laughed at himself for being so excited about a cheeseburger but he figured he'd earned this one. As he walked he considered where he might stay the night, whether he could hitch a ride and pick up his bike first. Would it fire? Did his club brother maintain it and start it occasionally, which was the deal? Of course everything would be good. One thing any Doomsayers MC patch holder could do was maintain a Harley. It would be exactly where it should be, full tank, and clean; there would be no questioning that, he could be sure. Three years inside for not rolling over on several other club members had enshrined

James in the DMC hall of fame. It meant little to him now but back then it meant everything.

A major condition of his parole was no association with the Doomsayers MC for one year. This was state stuff, non-negotiable. He would have to figure out how to live outside of a lifestyle which had consumed a decade. Ten years ago, after the death of his father and six months later his wife, both from cancer, James had reached the point where there was no point. He'd always ridden motorcycles and the helpless and hopeless existence pushed him further from normalcy or what most people consider normal. A family, job, house payment, birthdays and anniversaries, turkey dinners, and stockings hung on the mantle. Nothing wrong with those things — in fact, much is right about them — but after the endless sickness and eventual suffering and death he'd witnessed, nothing mattered anymore. He found himself in bars and with people he never would have spent time with before. Gravitational pull; misery loves company. The desperate and forgotten create their own orbit like a parallel universe sharing the same time-space continuum with the regular folks, but little else. James found himself frequenting a rustic biker bar just off the freeway on the outskirts of San Bernardino mastering their pool tables on a nightly basis, finding solace in classic rock and cold beer.

He had struggled to stay sober when his wife was alive, and he had made a promise to her that meant nothing to him after her death. He felt abandoned by her and by God. The pain was never satisfied but could at least be placed on hold in that environment. It wasn't until years later in the despair of prison that he learned onto whom he could unload that pain but oh, the damage done in the meantime! Each night disappearing into the next transcended weeks and then months and would have slowly consumed him had he not opted for a more expedient method of disaster.

The Doomsayers Motorcycle Club —or DMC to which they were notoriously referred by the police — and others of more dubious association fancied the Badlands Bar and Grill the perfect location for a local hang out. The bartenders, reconnaissance agents all, had good things to report when asked about the guy shooting pool every night. He kept to himself, tipped well, and said very little. He rode a Harley but nothing about him looked like a R.U.B. (rich urban biker). He wore jeans, boots, and a plain black t-shirt most nights and nothing advertising the famous Milwaukee, Wisconsin motorcycle company. He loved the bikes, not the "bling." The DMC liked that about him. James kept his distance, bought a few rounds and purposely lost a few games of pool during the first few months of 2001. He gained the DMC's acceptance by his steadfast show of respect. What happened on a hot Tuesday night in July would cement that trust.

The sex appeal of a biker bar or any good bar is the atmosphere. A good tavern can be expected to maintain a pitch, an environment of consistency, while offering the feeling that things could explode at any moment, some nights more than others. Like an airport walkway geared to move faster than normal pace, a good watering hole should feel like you've stepped from the pedestrian pace of everyday life onto the moving walkway of Margaritaville. Reality is still reality, but it's *out there* and it will be waiting for you when you return. Inside it's community, a family, and although we can talk smack among ourselves, God forbid an outsider dare advance without authorization. These establishments have eyes like the neighborhood watch. Bartenders, doormen, waitresses, and 'regulars' habitually monitor crowd movement and behavior and the seasoned among them can spot a potential problem a mile away.

The Badlands' layout was favorable for brawls with the pool tables separated from the main room only by a waist-high railing of varnished wood with high stools planted for viewing and waiting for an open table. The long similarly lacquered wood bar faced a large room with a dozen high tables and chairs that bordered a large dance floor and amplified juke box brimming with classic rock and blues from The Allman Brothers to ZZ Top.

Visibility was excellent from anywhere in the place. The young lady behind the bar had two doorbell type buttons on either end of the underside of the bar which, when pushed, lit red lights that alerted the bouncer and the manager to a potential situation. The fight on July

18th, 2001, was half over before she could hit either button.

At 7 p.m. James was holding court in the pool area with two DMC patch holders. Two more patch holders were at the end of the bar chatting up a couple of local lovelies. A couple of regulars populated the bar, but only six tables of other patrons were drinking and eating. Maybe it was the time of evening, or that it was still very bright outside on that hot summer night, but nobody thought it strange that two of the six tables each contained four men that nobody knew. Easier to judge after the fact, but these were not details which should have been missed, at least by the mix of employees and regular customers unlucky enough to be at the Badlands that early evening.

Four of the men began a clumsy game of doubles pool at the table adjacent to James and 'Scratch.' Sun Tzu would have recognized that the combatants then divided, flanked and positioned themselves behind their intended targets. Eight on four were great odds. On paper this would be an obvious mismatch, but these potential victims had been to other rodeos; they were outlaw bikers, after all. A fair fight would have ended badly for the attackers, but an orchestrated surprise caught the victims unaware and ill prepared. The eight attacked the four with everything available. Beer bottles, cue sticks, and fists. It's one thing when two guys are, 'oh yeahing,' each other and tempers and awareness escalate, but quite another when it comes immediately and seemingly without provocation. All four DMC members were bloody and down with Scratch slumped against a tall chair, the pool table separating him from James, struggling to regain his faculties. The attackers were already moving toward the door when the first ball hit and downed the tallest guy, two more balls, a thud and a loud crack dropped the two men who had turned to see what had felled their lead man. James drew his leg up and snapped his cue stick in half, grabbed another ball and ran directly at the five men, cracking the slowest guy in the face with his stick. He stood over him and hit him three more times directly in the nose and then came straight up and clothes-lined the next slowest guy across the neck with the stick end.

He then smashed the nine ball into the man's teeth, breaking as many as he could as fast as he could.

This sent the remaining attackers running out the door. James yelled a deep guttural scream and ran after all of them, tackling the closest of the sprinters. According to the doorman, who had grabbed another of the guys as two of the recovering patch holders came running out, James tackled the guy and then lifted him by his long hair and began repeatedly smashing the guy's face into his knee until the crowd came out and pulled him off. His victim collapsed in the gravel. The other two guys jumped into a waiting pickup truck and sped off, filling the summer evening with gravel and dust. The bouncer tossed his Jeep keys to the two DMCs and they sped off after the pickup truck. Somebody called 911— not the cops but an ambulance — as two of the attackers and one DMC were in pretty bad shape and there was some fear that one or more of them might die on the spot. That would be bad for the insurance rates.

Just as fire brings smoke, an ambulance comes with cops, especially at the Badlands. And they showed up fast! Seven San Bernardino Sheriff's units converged on the parking lot with guns drawn and ordered everyone on the ground. James resisted their requests and was taken down by two officers in spite of the bouncer's insistence that he did nothing but defend himself and others. After several minutes of discussion and the testimony of several customers, the deputies released James who brushed the dirt from his shirt and jeans and ran his fingers through his tangled, sweaty hair. He had a way of looking at you that could chill your blood. Not menacing, necessarily, just a focused gaze with sharp eyes. It was the look of a man who had forgotten how to feel anything but rage. The deputies kept a close eye on him as they assessed the damage and injuries. One cop asked James if he needed to go to the hospital.

"I'm fine," he shot back.

The paramedics emerged from the bar with three gurneys bouncing in the gravel and dirt, which makes up most of the parking lot.

"Hey! Take it easy," James barked. "This guy don't need your freaking help if you're gonna bounce him to the hospital," as he pointed to 'Hammer,' the DMC in the horizontal carrier.

"Shut up," shot a deputy.

"Screw you," James hissed in a tone that made even the deputy leave it alone. There had been an amazing fight and he didn't seem to care one bit if it went on for a few more minutes with some cops. "Can I go now?" he asked.

"Yeah, just don't leave town anytime soon; we'll have some more questions," one cop said. James just shrugged and headed back inside.

The Doomsayers MC Treasurer, Scratch, was sitting on a bar stool staring at the jukebox when James walked in. Several people in the doorway moved aside as he entered. Some were muttering their admiration as James beelined to Scratch, who turned on his stool to face James. "You alright, man?" James asked the biker.

"Man, that was freaking nuts what you did back there, bro; ain't nobody gonna forget that craziness." He raised his arm and clasped James' hand and hugged him.

James tilted his head and looked at Scratch's badly cut left temple and and bruised upper cheek and asked if he was okay or if he should go with his brother, Hammer, to the hospital.

"No, man, I'm okay, just a head wound; anyplace else woulda killed me!" They both thought that was funny.

"Who were those idiots; you have any idea?" James asked.

"No clue, bro, but they ain't gonna get away from Offramp and Panhead. Those two will chase those fools into the night and leave 'em out there. No doubt somebody don't like us, maybe another club, I don't know, but we will find out and we will even this up. But I'm tellin' you, bro, that stunt you pulled was righteous; you are down! There's gonna be some brothers gonna want to pay respects. Snake already called and said he was coming down."

James just nodded; he neither needed nor wanted recognition. He had a life once, a wife with whom he had planned a family, a good job, all the ingredients, but that was all gone now and with it went his concern for approval. He was just going through the motions trying to stay reasonably sane in a messed-up world. His sobriety meant something once. Not so much now. He ordered a beer but when he pushed a five-spot over the bar he was informed his money was no good there that night.

"Well, then, Samantha, I'll take the lobster as well," to which she replied with a wink, "You don't want the seafood here."

He took the cold beer and headed back to the solace of the pool table. If Snake (the Mother Chapter President or "the P") was heading over, James knew he'd be staying late. He could already hear the sound of several motorcycles pulling into the parking lot. Word travels fast and his legend was quickly forged by the many witnesses. By virtue of his participation, James had just entered into a world of violent drama and intensity the likes of which he'd never imagined. There would be no turning back.

~

"Hi, can I take your order?" a voice so sweet and innocent it shattered his flashback. He couldn't even remember the last half mile or so but he had obviously arrived at his intended destination.

"Yeah, just a number one with grilled onions and light sauce, add mustard and pickles; for here, please," was his automatic response. He chuckled inside — *some things never change* — paid his six dollars and change and took his receipt — number eighty four — as number fifty-one was being called over the loudspeaker. He knew from experience that the normal wait was about seven minutes, but with thirty-three orders in front of him and many of them drive thru, it might stretch into the nine-minute range. He wondered how many people had calculated their average burger preparation time. He reasoned that since they noted the order time on the receipt it was perfectly within his purview to note the stop time as well and then commit it to memory to be retrieved each time he ordered a burger and thus arrive at an average cook time. Whatever, he was fifty for Pete's sake; he determined the chances of his changing this strange behavior were poor and ultimately unimportant.

Eight minutes and forty seconds later he was marveling over a wonderfully presented double cheeseburger with fries and a very cold coke with a lemon slice. It looked awesome. In-N-Out enthusiasts will agree that it takes approximately half the time to eat these things as it does to prepare them. Oh well, he thought, it's worth every minute! The dinner gave him ample time to relax and regroup as he prepared his mind for the coming day. He used his new phone to make contact with his old friends Marc, not affiliated with DMC so a safe call, and his wife, Robin, both overjoyed to hear his voice. They insisted that he at least spend the night and would be there to pick him up in forty-five minutes. James loved his friends and thought that Marc was crazier than any DMC, but the state knew best. *Some guys just never get caught*, he thought as he headed back to the cashier.

"Vanilla shake, please; no lid, no straw." It was the perfect dessert. James always ordered the milkshakes with no lid and no straw because he considered it ridiculous to work while eating dessert and trying to draw an In-N-Out milkshake through a straw was freaking work! He much preferred to gulp the frozen bliss and enjoy massive globs of icy vanilla rather than the aerobic exhaustion of coaxing cubic centimeters from the cup regardless of the extended time the straw provided. Yes, he'd thought about this before. He discovered that In-N-Out had seen fit to print Bible scripture addresses on the inside bottom ring of every cup. His milkshake cup rocked Proverbs 3:6. He'd never noticed this before and the revelation made him smile. No wonder you never see a boarded-up In-N-Out.

James considered another milkshake but only for a fleeting moment. He thought better of it as he remembered the only other time he opted for two milkshakes. He was on a run with the DMC and it was crazy hot through San Fernando Valley and after the second shake he was in agony for twenty miles. *Never mind*, he thought, *never again*. His thoughts ran to Gary, his new trucker buddy and how, why, James never found a moment during their almost eight hour association to mention God. He likened this reflection to a sports team that after a loss — or victory for that matter — spent time breaking down film. What could he have done better? How would he react the next time? James knew that in the Bible, Jesus instructed his disciples to *tell people about me*; it's referred to as the Great Commission and its message is to all believers, not just the disciples. It is the heart and soul of evangelism. James remembered another scripture: *If you are ashamed of me, my Father in heaven will be ashamed of you.* There is a world of difference between the conviction from God and the condemnation from the enemy. The Bible also says, *There is therefore now no condemnation to those who are in Christ Jesus, who do not walk according to the flesh, but according to the Spirit.* Romans 8:1.

Feeling bad that he had not taken an opportunity to share the gospel with Gary, James needed to discern the difference, learn from it, move on, and not wallow in the feeling of failure, which was the enemy's goal. God says, *I love you, let's keep going,* and the enemy says, *You suck; quit.* Did he feel ill-equipped to share this belief that had changed a raging violent man into a patient and peaceful ambassador for Christ? If so, why? Was he afraid of Gary's reaction? If a salesman is supremely confident in his product, he will share its opportunity to anyone and everyone. Did James lack this confidence? *Shake it off,* James thought. Move on. *You'll have other opportunities to avail yourself to the Lord. You are forgiven; you are not doomed.*

# Chapter Six

"Jaammes." Marc's voice was unmistakable. Forty years removed from Chicago had no effect on that Midwest accent. Marc's arm quickly head-locked James before he could exit the restaurant booth. Robin was thrilled to see him, but then Robin was always thrilled ... about everything. She was the joy that balanced Marc's manic moods. She was Yang or Yin and he was the other guy. Better friends could not be had. Loyal and down, no matter how crazy things got and years ago, the crazier the better. They never shrank from backing a brother's play. As crazy as Marc was in his earlier years, he was the voice of reason that James ignored when the DMC came courting that fateful summer. He always told James that when you patch in a club you inherit every problem the club has, every public or private issue haunting every member becomes your problem. What you don't know *can* hurt you. To Marc's credit, he never said, 'I told you so,' and he certainly had opportunity for that.

"You just couldn't wait to eat here, could you?" Robin said kiddingly. James smiled and shrugged that 'you know' shrug she loved. Much about him was loveable in a stray dog kind of way. The ride to their home was filled with laughter and stories about old friends and acquaintances.

James was glad to be with friends again, the past three years having been spent on constant alert. In prison there was never any real peace and deep down James was a peaceful man. "I found the Lord in prison and I got licensed and ordained," James blurted out.

"Why was the Lord in prison?" Marc blurted out, and they all had a good laugh. "Everyone gets religion in prison, bro," he added.

"Yeah, I know, but something happened to me in there, bro; this is real."

Robin broke the tension, "Well, I think it's great; you'll make a great preacher."

"Thanks, Mom," Marc teased.

"Shut up, Marc; I'm serious. If this is what he wants, then good for him."

James thought they had forgotten he was in the minivan with them as they argued back and forth. He knew that Marc was a devout pagan dog who had been raised Catholic but associated God with a mean guy sporting a white beard just tapping his foot waiting for us to sin so he could blast us with his cosmic ruler across the hands. James knew this would be a sore subject, but he was determined to get it out in the open and not shrink from the discussion. Marc loved James regardless of his beliefs but as with many people, he was so invested in his agnostic philosophy that his pride would not let him entertain anything else. James had thought long and hard about this pride-versus-faith struggle and had determined that this struggle caused most problems in the world. Pride and faith — it was always too much of one and not enough of the other. Wars, family feuds, broken relationships, estranged friendships everything can be traced back to pride and faith.

James changed the subject. "Hey, bro, can we swing by Berdoo real quick? I'd like to pick up my bike. It's at a parking structure up the 215 north off of 2nd street; it won't take long."

"You still have the bike?" Robin asked.

"Of course he still has the bike, Robin; he'd sell off everything else but not the black beauty!" Marc snapped.

James again felt like he wasn't in the vehicle, only this time it was uncomfortable. He sensed some strain in Marc's voice. "Dude, seriously, if it's out of your way, just shine it; I'll get it tomorrow."

"Not at all, man. I'm just messing with you; of course we can get your bike. I'm sure after three years it needs to be ridden! You're still comin to the house, right?" Marc added.

James realized that Marc's manic swing might be attributed to the thought that James was just using them for a ride and responded, teasing, "Of course, if you'll still have me!"

"I'll think about it. The dogs might attack you … they hate Christians!" Marc chuckled, amused at his own comments.

"O.M.G., Marc! You are so rude."

"That's part of his charm and that's why you love him so much," James said. He was relieved that the conversation had returned, the ice of three years removed, and the associated bad memories were thawing a bit. James reached in his pockets for his bike keys once again, needing the peace that the unmistakable feel of the barrel key brought him. He thought about what Marc had said about riding the bike again and it filled him with the urge to feel that beast under him.

He'd ridden over forty thousand miles on that bike. Miles that at times were serene and effortless, and others, at terrifyingly high speed insanity on the outer fringes of the laws of physics. His Harley was his only real possession and he'd sleep on a wet bank under a bridge before he'd sell it. James was holding the vision of his bike as the 'pinch me' moment of his trip back to Southern California. He had no reason to think that the bike was not there; his former club owed him that much for sure, but he needed to see it with his own eyes and most importantly, touch it before he'd finally relax and trust that he was indeed free again.

Sure, there was parole and he'd need to check in with his agent but that was only for one year, some special dispensation from the Pope, or the D.A.; he wasn't sure, but his slick attorney had insisted that it was a great deal and to show some respect and appreciation to the district attorney for the easy parole. *Screw them*, James thought. That political hack had jammed him up at the trial, trying to introduce RICO statutes, organized crime connections— you name it — he was more interested in his rising career than the facts of the case. James had forgiven him but he wasn't about to buy him lunch and thank him for the great deal. *I ain't that saved*, James laughed to himself. "Yeah, bro, off here and hang a right; it's by the Carousel Mall. I can't believe that dump is still open."

"They put it at the mall?" Marc asked incredulously.

"No, it's in a city ramp across from the mall right behind that congressman's office at 2nd and E Street. One of the brothers works there and told his bosses it was his bike ... whatever. As long as it's there, I'm cool." replied James.

Marc rolled the black minivan slowly to the lowering red and white striped barrier. He pushed the lighted green button and retrieved the parking ticket and placed it on his dash. As James stuck a five dollar bill over the front seat he was met with stinging slap to the top of his hand. "Owww," he said.

"That's what you get. Don't you insult me with that; don't bring that up here, James Walters!" Robin scolded.

"Dang, sorry; okay," he answered.

"Screw that; give me the money," Marc said, laughing.

"Maybe later, brother, when she goes to bed ... that freaking hurt," James whined.

"Oh, man up. I'm sure by the looks of you, it was tougher inside than a little hand slap," Robin teased.

"Thanks a lot," he pouted.

"Is that it up there on the right side next to that yellow pole?" Marc asked.

"Freaking bike better not have any yellow on it," James voice tailed off. There was a somewhat undersized dusty cover draped over the bike that left the rear hard bags exposed. Black and shiny but exposed, which led James to think that it had recently been cleaned. As emotionally distant as James was from the outlaw world he recognized and appreciated that show of respect, but was a bit put off by the downsized sized bike cover on his Street Glide. At least it was somewhat covered. James climbed out the sliding side door and verified the license plate and the current tags. "That's what I'm talking about," James said. "This is righteous."

"It's the least they could do after ..." Marc stopped as James shot him a look that said no further comment was necessary.

James carefully pulled the cover back like he was unveiling a delicate statue. The echo of approaching footsteps caused James to look down the ramp at three guys heading their way. "Get away from that bike," one of them yelled.

"Screw you!" Marc yelled back.

James quietly instructed Marc, "Tell them "Nine Ball is picking up his bike."

Marc looked toward the men whose pace had quickened and noted one had a chain and the others had 'chuks and he declared, "Nine Ball is picking up his bike!"

All three men stopped mid-stride. One of them called out, "No disrespect but I have to ask; do you know what time it is?"

James whispered to Marc, 'Tulsa time,' whereby Marc yelled, "Tulsa time!"

The men turned without a word and walked away. "Tulsa time?" Marc laughed and shook his head.

"It's not that long of a story, bro, we just needed a password and I can't be anywhere near any DMC for a year. We settled on 'Tulsa time,' so thanks for interpreting for us." Marc just slowly shook his head.

The massive motorcycle rumbled like only a 103 cubic inch V twin with upgraded cams can rumble. James smiled to himself as he unfolded and read the note taken from between the seat and gas tank. He sat and listened to his bike. The Doomsayers MC had taken some time and a considerable amount of money to make some modifications to the engine and exhaust and it sounded like a symphony. In this parking structure, the noise wasn't just loud, it was thunderous. He was quite moved by the gesture and couldn't wait to get this thing on the highway.

"I'd say follow us home but you won't and you already know the way!" Marc laughed.

"The key's in the usual place if you're really late," Robin added.

"I'll be there shortly after you guys. No worries, bro; thanks again."

Marc knew it might be much later that evening when his old buddy would roll up to his front door, but he was happy to be a part of this reunion. He didn't know anyone who loved to ride more than J.W. and figured that three years in the joint might cause him to roll for quite awhile before he found Moreno Valley some twelve miles south. James could roll to Palm Desert to buy a cigar and ride back again later for a lighter. He was that nuts! And that's why Marc loved him; heck, that's why everyone loved him. He did what most people only think of doing. And truth be told, he did some things most people wouldn't believe anyone could do. At least he used to. Who knew what this Jesus trip was all about; maybe he was done with crazy. Yeah, sure he was.

James watched as Marc and Robin slowly drove out of the parking structure. They were good friends for sure and he appreciated the ride. In the thirty years that he and Marc were friends, James had never seen Marc on a bike. He was more of a Detroit muscle car guy; he had a big long yellow Mustang when they first met, a 429, he thought it was. That car got both of them in plenty of trouble. Marc was still paying their attorney ten years after he shook those charges. Greenberg was a great lawyer; James should stop by and say hello now that he was out. He had a payment plan with him, too!

He smiled. They used to joke that together they were making Greenberg's Ferrari payments. Probably were.

James thought he might ride east on the 10 freeway just to get out to Yucaipa and up through Cherry Valley. He'd be careful not to exit at Live Oak Boulevard this time. Maybe just roll out to Beaumont, tag up, take the split and ride back on the 60 freeway through the pass down to Moreno Valley. Forty-five miles that route or twelve miles down the 215 freeway. *Take the long way home.*

He smiled to himself as he opened his hard plastic saddle bags to locate his leather and his gloves. It had to be in the fifties still, but it sure as heck would get crazy cold through the pass. James laughed as he remembered riding through that very canyon with only a leather vest freezing his butt off a few years ago. *No thanks*, he thought. *I am older and wiser now, praise God.* He uttered a little prayer in his head. A prayer of thanks for his freedom and his bike and whatever the Lord had in store.

He pulled a leg over the seat, taking care as always not to scuff the bags with his boots. *There's nothing like this*, he thought and smiled as he noticed the red needle pegged to the "F" position in the lighted fuel gauge. James nodded to himself in a salute to his club. He let out the clutch and set off every car alarm in the place.

## Chapter Seven

The combination of the engine work and the three-year hiatus produced a wide smile, the kind that stays for awhile. The motorcycle's power and noticeably improved acceleration was glorious! James' only concern now was getting to the freeway before the cops heard that bike. He had never been pulled over on the freeway. For some reason the various west coast Highway Patrol had always given him a wide berth, even when flying the notorious Doomsayers MC colors at high speeds throughout their four-state stomping grounds. When James was sentenced, the DMC was active in Oregon, California, Nevada, and Arizona. Local cops and sheriffs were a different story, as he and his brothers had been repeatedly harassed by several jurisdictions for loud pipes and other violations involving exhibitions of speed and assorted recklessness. Greenberg had been largely successful in defending him against these annoyances, but it never stopped the locals from pulling him over and playing twenty questions.

He entered the southbound 215 freeway redlining second, third, and fourth gear before backing off and settling into fifth at eighty-five mph, weaving his way through the light-to-medium southbound traffic. James knew to back her down to seventy or so as he made the transition to Interstate 10 freeway eastbound, where he wound the bike back to one hundred, gliding over the three lanes necessary to gain entrance to the carpool lane, which was sparsely traveled this evening. James laughed out loud as he settled in at eighty where this new engine seemed to thrive. It was fantastic! The bike moved better than he remembered and James reasoned that the club must have altered the handling characteristics as well as the engine. It was appreciated.

His initial thought was to ride to Phoenix but he quickly remembered that unauthorized crossing of state lines would be a parole violation and thought better of it. He laughed to himself that his earlier thirty-five mph over the posted limit might give pause to his parole officer, but some things were unavoidable. Without sounding like a Harley commercial, suffice it to say the bike effortlessly made the Redlands to Yucaipa grade in fifth gear. James glanced periodically in his mirror only to see pavement pouring out from behind him in the headlights of the cars as he passed them one after another along the dark highway. This was freedom.

His past, like those headlights, was all behind him and only God's best lay ahead for him. He felt his spirit soar as the digital odometer racked up miles like a pinball machine scoreboard. He would have to get some word of appreciation to DMC for this great welcome home present.

James negotiated the big bike off the highway at Beaumont Avenue and made both lights before another high speed entrance to the 10 freeway, westbound this time. As he always made the fast lane his home; the transition to the westbound 60 was gentle even at eighty miles per hour. Ahead of him was about a fifteen mile run through some great canyon highway, but he had to keep an eye out for the occasional slow movers. This stretch was significantly less forgiving than the westbound Interstate 10 with only half the navigable lanes on which to ride. No street lights for miles, just the moonlight, which was ample in its last quarter this time of the month. James and his bike settled in between seventy and eighty through the pass, enjoying the long sweeping curves and mile-long straightaways before the long straight between Pigeon Pass and Day Street where he would reluctantly exit and rejoin civilization in the struggling middle class expanse known as Moreno Valley.

James opened the bike up completely in the last two miles, then had to shut it down at one hundred and fifteen as he was nearing his exit. It had much more to offer but he'd let her run again in a day or so when he planned to ride to Palm Desert. There was a wonderful cigar lounge at 'The River,' a ritzy shopping and restaurant area built with a manmade waterway coursing through its center. He reasoned that he couldn't do everything in one night and he was exhausted after a very long first day.

He rolled as quietly as possible up the neighborhood street, passing dozens of duplicate houses, each with three or four cars in the driveways and overflowing to the street. To get to Marc and Robin's house it was necessary to negotiate a veritable maze of streets and there was no quick exit. Michelle would have called this neighborhood an ant farm. He really missed her sense of humor. James thought that Marc must have softened his legendary paranoia to have chosen such a place. Outlaw housing should always be situated in an isolated but highly accessible location, with excellent visibility. This place reflected none of those characteristics, but there were some nice rose bushes and neatly manicured shrubs leading to the front door.

James managed a wry smile thinking that he might never quite fit into society, but that didn't necessarily bother him. He considered walking right in but the barking of several large-sounding dogs made him rethink that plan. He knocked. Robin, surrounded by dogs, answered the door. "Well, come on in. We didn't think you'd show till much later," she laughed and hugged him again like it had been nine years, not ninety minutes since they last spoke. "Marc's in back with Demon."

"With who?" asked James.

"Demon; he's seventy percent wolf and he's awesome. Marc is crazy about him."

"He's crazy, all right," answered James, shaking his head.

"Come on you sissy, you'll love him; you love dogs."

"Dogs, yes, wolves, not so much," he muttered. "Nice roses by the way," he said.

"Screw you, James," she said looking straight ahead as she led the way through the kitchen. "Marc!" she yelled. "Your Christian friend is here."

"Touché," he joked.

"I don't have any Christian friends; get rid of him," Marc yelled back.

"He's really happy you're out," Robin whispered to James.

"I can tell," he said and they both smiled.

James stood at the sliding glass door gazing out to the patio where his friend was entertaining what looked very much like a wolf. Marc motioned for James to come outside. *Why me*, James thought as he slowly slid the door open and just as slowly stepped out. It was a beautiful night with a light warm breeze, which James would have appreciated had his gaze not been locked on the wolf dog. Demon was breathtakingly beautiful in a *Call of the Wild* sort of way. He was wildly magnificent, athletic and very strong. He pulled Marc's two hundred pound frame like a child's little red wagon and it was quite clear that Demon wanted to smell or eat James' leather jacket. Marc was as excited as a child about this animal. Evidently Robin, in her inimitable fashion, talked the breeder out of this monster after Marc had expressed a maniacal interest the first time he laid eyes on the then shoebox-sized pup. They had five other dogs and at least seven cats and a Burmese Python somewhere, presumably in an aquarium upstairs.

"Aren't you worried he will eat the cats?" James asked.

"They're Robin's cats," Marc laughed, feigning indifference. "Nah, we keep him out here most of time and I built him a big house next to the garage. He loves it over there. Bro, you should hear him howl; it's freaking awesome!" Marc continued.

"I can't wait ... is he going to eat my arm?" James asked nervously as the wolf gnawed on his right forearm.

"Maybe. I've never seen him do that," offered Marc.

James was hoping the human chew toy game was not one of those bluffs gone awry.

"Where's your faith?" Marc taunted.

"Oh, my prayer life has gotten stronger the last few minutes, I'll tell you that!" James threw back.

"Seriously, bro, do you think God's gonna save you from Demon?" Marc looked up from his kneeling position, hugging the wolf.

James responded, "Maybe ... the Bible says we have an appointed time to die. If this is it, then no, but if it's not, I'll walk out of here.

"Hmmm, so however you end up dying, you think God kills you?" Marc continued.

"I think God will allow something to end my life when it's His time. It ain't gonna catch Him by surprise but I don't think He goes around killing people. Jeez, brother, I don't know," James laughed. "He's God, man, He can do whatever He wants. I trust Him, though; that's the big difference for me now, I guess," he added.

"That's cool, bro; whatever works for you," Marc said.

James saw a slight opening. "Nah, bro, it's not whatever works for me, it's truth and if it's truth then it has to be truth for everyone. I don't believe for one minute in relative truth. I think the 'whatever works for you' crap is a copout; I don't believe the Lord left that as a viable option.

"Ah, you think your way is the only way?" Marc challenged.

"It's not my way, it's His way. Jesus himself said that He was the way, the truth and the life and that no one can come to the Father but by the son, so it's God's way."

Marc answered, "Well, I don't like that your way or whatever you just said is the only way; it's too exclusive a club. I don't subscribe to that."

"Yeah, a lot of people feel the same way. I used to as well."

"What changed?" Marc wondered.

"I started to figure that by thinking that way I was dictating how God had to do things, and by acting like that I was telling 'God' what to do and how to do it and I realized that I had screwed my life up by my decisions, so if I was acting like a little god and messing everything up, who was I to tell God anything?" James finished and they both laughed.

"Good point; you are a first-class screw up!" Marc added loudly.

"Word," James said.

"You guys want a beer or anything?" Robin yelled from the kitchen.

"Great idea," Marc yelled back.

"Not for me; I'll take a glass of water or something," James replied.

"Oh, jeez, here we go," Marc said to no one in particular. "Are you on the wagon again? I thought for sure you'd want a cold keg of Bass Ale the day you got out."

"Yeah, I really haven't given it much thought. I just don't have the desire anymore," James said.

"Really?" Marc asked, and it sounded like "reeeelly."

James just smiled at his buddy and said, "Reeeelly," and they both laughed. Marc put his arm around his friend and led him from the patio to the kitchen.

"No beer for you?" Robin asked.

"It's a miracle from God!" Marc blurted out. Everyone laughed and James was relieved that the harassment appeared to be minimal and at least for the night, ended.

"Did you get out this morning?" Robin asked, changing the subject as she handed James a tall ice water.

"Yeah, like 3:45 this morning. It was hard to believe that it was finally over, that I was actually done, but I was a little nervous until I cleared that old gate!" James said.

"It went by fast ... for us!" Marc added, laughing again.

"Well, I'm glad to hear that you had such an easy time of it," James responded jovially.

Unwilling to let it go, Marc replied, "Me, too!"

They moved to the living room where the conversation lightened with Marc sharing how much he hated his job as an operations manager with a large trucking company and how someday they'd have an internet business that would allow him to quit. It was a dream he'd had for years and no amount of, 'You should be happy you have a job in this economy,' type of talk would satisfy his burning desire for something better, or more importantly, different.

James was struggling to stay awake at this hour. It was nearing eleven and he'd covered a lot of miles, and with the help of Gary and these two friends, accomplished a great deal in one day. As Robin talked about her recent volunteer work at a local animal rescue shelter, she noticed that their house guest was nodding off and offered the spare bedroom down the hall, which James enthusiastically accepted.

Then, to his surprise, Marc indicated that he'd like to continue their earlier conversation if James was up to more questioning the next evening. Robin was curious, too, so James invited both of them to dinner. A deal was struck and James headed down the hall to a soft bed and visions of his first uninterrupted night's sleep in three years. He prayed a thankful prayer and asked God to give him the words needed for the next day's discussion.

James figured he would take some time in the morning and ride to the bank where his sister had set up his account and then cruise around looking at potential industrial property to rent where he could re-establish a motorcycle shop with decent exposure. He had until the end of next week to establish contact with his parole officer so no need to rush that meeting. He was quite sure he could kill most of the day following those simple pursuits. Oh, and find a good gym; he'd need a place to pump some iron, otherwise the In-N-Out's would in time erode his chiseled physique. He took a deep breath. This had been a great day.

Chapter Eight

James awoke to the joyous sound of song birds outside his window that was open just enough for the warm breeze to fill the room. It took him a good five seconds to realize where he was and what day it was, such was his early degree of confusion. It wasn't euphoria, but it was close. One doesn't appreciate the taste of freedom quite like the person to whom such freedom has been denied. He lay there for several minutes in prayer and appreciation before heading down the hall to the first non-regulated shower in three years.

After washing off the grime of the previous day, James visited the kitchen where a pot of coffee had just brewed, courtesy of a timer. There was a note on the counter from Robin wishing him a great second day of freedom and her anticipation of dinner plans. James jotted his new phone number on the note and invited a call later in the day to firm up a time and choice of restaurant. He helped himself to the bag of steel cut oatmeal and located the brown sugar in the cabinet above the coffee maker. This oatmeal was a far cry from the watered-down gruel he had eaten every morning for the past three years. The addition of brown sugar was pure bliss; the third teaspoon might have bordered on decadent but he couldn't think of a better way to start the day. He considered eating outside but the possibility of facing the wolf alone was more adventure than he needed this early in the day. He sat at the counter and ate every last bit of that bowl before he washed and dried his morning dishes. *No prints, no evidence*, he said to himself.

Already midday warm by eight forty-five, James rolled his jacket and gloves into a ball and stuffed them into his hard plastic saddle bags. He slid his Ray Bans into place, then quickly clicked the chin strap on his 'not quite' D.O.T. approved helmet and quickly patted his jeans to ensure his wallet and cell phone were secure. As the bike thundered to life, James determined a route that would eventually lead to the Bank of America in Colton where his sister had opened his account. He had the manager's business card crammed into his wallet ... somewhere. No matter, really; he was sure a quick check of his identification would yield the account information. The real reason he was riding to the Colton address instead of a closer branch was that his sister had mentioned that the bank manager was beautiful ... and single ... and he wanted a closer look. *You're quite a catch,* he laughed to himself.

City riding was the worst. It was something to be tolerated enroute to the highway where a guy could ask some things of his bike. Highways in California at 9:00 a.m., however, were another story altogether. Most mornings are like scenes from *Mad Max*. Cars, trucks, rigs, all jockey for position during the earlier part of the day, but after nine conditions morph into higher speeds and missed appointments. In the early hours people are zombies with greasy fast food breakfasts and precariously balanced scalding coffee, but the nine-to-noon crowd is cell phones and car seats, a more dangerous animal indeed from a biker viewpoint. Early morning drivers are psychotic, but they are highly skilled; mid-morning soccer moms and inattentive sales reps are pure evil.

James hit the 60 freeway west at fifty miles an hour and began the slalom course through Moreno Valley and Riverside before the transition to the death race up the 215 north to Interstate 10 west. Traffic moved fairly well, the radio guys call it 'Friday light,' as for some strange reason fewer people seem to work on Fridays in Southern California than the other four days. James had upgraded the stereo system on his motorcycle, as music was the backdrop to everything in his life. An amplifier was stuffed into the fairing, which fed the intricate speaker system — all leading to an FM/CD/MP3 deck and the morning's selection, "Tales of Great Ulysses" by Cream. Prison with a great stereo system would have been almost tolerable, but there was very little in the way of quality music in that place. It was 9:20 a.m. and he was singing along at the top of his lungs. He must have looked like a complete idiot white-lining through traffic twenty miles per hour faster than anyone else and singing "while his naked ears were tortured," loudly out of tune, but he never gave it a second thought. The dude was in his element.

James was encouraged to see several dozen 'For Lease' signs on what appeared to be excellent candidates for the type of building he had in mind.

Fifteen hundred or so square feet with a small office and larger warehouse/shop space in back with a roll-up door. Three years ago rents were considerably higher, so there was something to say for a depressed economy when shopping for space. He quickly figured he'd be able to secure suitable accommodations in any one of a dozen or more areas for somewhere around fifty cents a square foot, which was a considerable savings over what he'd previously paid. His mood was upbeat as he rolled west and daydreamed about a thriving motorcycle shop with a pool table and some classic rock playing in the background. No hip hop; he had paid his debt to society.

He hadn't thought much about it the night before, but it dawned on him right away that morning that he felt naked without his colors. As a DMC patch holder and the Mother Chapter's Road Captain, he had never ridden without his 'cut,' but as a condition of his parole, any outward sign of his former affiliation — his vest (cut) with the 'rocker' patch that read 'West Shore' identifying the DMC's territory, his colors, which is a high honor and members have and will continue to die to protect — were off limits for the time being.

He had risen quickly in the ranks that summer's night, basically bypassing the two levels of protocol of all outlaw motorcycle clubs. But no Mother Chapter member had any objections to the monumental move of patching him in after James' participation that night, knowing him from the frequent pool games, and his uncanny ability to diagnose and fix Harleys. He was not given 'hang around' status, the initial and unofficial starting point — an unglorified gopher expected to serve the club and say nothing until a club determines you're not a complete moron and you may have what it takes to be a full member some day. Having already proven his value, the club didn't even bother giving him the title of 'prospect,' or glorified gopher, which bordered on indentured servitude, the only thing worse being a 'hang around.' Nor did James have to wait the minimum six months to become, on the sponsorship of a full patch and a subsequent unanimous vote, a full Patch Holder.

James held DMC's Road Captain position in charge of all movement once "kickstands were up," along with maintenance of bikes and all navigation to and from club runs. Even the 'P' followed the Road Captain's instructions once the kickstands were up. Having spent his formative years in Michigan where his father had taught him boating and seamanship came in handy as club navigator and resident meteorologist.

James was riding his bike now stripped of that status and affiliation. It felt weird. He looked like any other motorcycle enthusiast out for a morning ride. No matter now that he was patched up by none other than Snake, the DMC "P" on the night after the Badlands' fight. James had never given them reason to pause, even refusing to "rat out" other members, which had earned him three years in Folsom prison for his silence. He was an outlaw legend on the West Coast. A whirlwind had vacuumed him in before he had a moment to consider, and in basking in the glory of his new fame, he had made a decision that forever labeled him an outlaw. Yet James never blamed anything that happened to him on anyone but himself. He believed strongly in something his father had taught him as a boy: 'The height of maturity is taking full responsibility for one's actions.'

Now, after a string of questionable decisions, he found himself climbing from his motorcycle at a bank in Colton, California, and walking inside to claim an inheritance left to him by the only person he'd ever call a saint. Starting right then, he intended to embark on a life that she would be proud to watch unfold. He knew he'd been called by God and even in prison was spared much pain that was meant for him. There were too many close calls to attribute to coincidence. He had seen God's hand at work and now this man would avail himself to that same God.

James entered the busy bank, helmet in one hand as the other fumbled through his wallet for Linda Stevenson's business card. Nobody acknowledged him, so he took a seat with several other customers around a short round worthless little table, the surface of which held several carvings courtesy, apparently, of past disgruntled visitors. He nervously handled the dog-eared business card like it was a ticket to an event. *You look like a psychotic homeless guy,* he thought. *No wonder they won't talk to you.*

He sat for a few minutes in silence, nodding and smiling to the other customers and then rose up from his chair and approached a twenty-something female employee with costume makeup wearing a black dress and brown shoes. Even James knew that was a fashion faux pas, but he figured she was doing the best that she could. Her name tag read, 'Hello, can I help you?' so calling her by name would be tough. "I need to check the status of my account, but I don't know the number," he said.

"Actually, any of our tellers would be happy to help you, sir," she answered.

"Is Linda here today?" he asked.

"Actually she is in a meeting right now," she said.

James thought it was idiotic to use 'actually' in every sentence, but he let it slide. "Okay, cool, I'll see a teller," he answered as politely as he could and took his place in line. Seven people in front of him, five tellers — make that four tellers — the large lady with the same makeup artist as "Hello, can I help you?" just closed her window. *Amazing*, he thought. James observed everyone in the bank all at once and determined that the fall of western civilization was at hand. He knew he should not judge, but dang, there were some ignorant people walking around. He then realized that if someone walked in and surveyed the clientele, he would appear as torn up as anyone in there. That was a humbling thought. *My day is going to crap*, he laughed to himself.

"I can help you," came the voice from the far left window.

He headed in that direction. "Clare, is it? How you doing today, Clare?" he asked.

"I'm fine. How can I help you?" she asked.

"My sister opened an account for me while I was ... I was out of town for a time. I don't have the account number, but I was told that if I showed you this, you could figure it out." He slipped the driver's license up through the little stainless steel half pipe and waited as she examined his license.

"This is you?" she asked.

"No, it's my sister … Yes, it's me," he replied, trying for a little levity. His charm wasn't working today.

"I show several accounts under James Walters. Do you have an address that I can reference?"

"I think it's a P.O. Box in Chino Hills," he answered. "There should be like seventeen-eight or so in the account, give or take some service charges," he offered.

"What are the last four numbers of your social?"

"Nine-one-three-four," he said.

"I show the account, a savings account opened a year ago last November. It's not the amount you mentioned, but I can print out your balance if you like."

"Yes, thank you." He wondered what she meant by 'not the amount you mentioned,' but that question was answered almost immediately when the printed slip was handed back to him along with his license. "This can't be right," he said, stunned by the amount: twenty-three forty-four and change. "There was almost eighteen grand in here," his voice trailed off.

"I see there was an opening balance of seventeen thousand eight hundred thirty-three dollars, but it looks like there was a deduction here in December for fifteen thousand six hundred sixty-seven and sixteen cents. There was some interest paid last December as well, but I don't know what to tell you except ... hold on a second, there's a code here ... it looks like the IRS levied the account for that money. I'm sorry, but we can't do anything when they do that," she explained.

"Is there anyone I can speak with?" he asked.

Clare looked nervously through the thick glass partition over his shoulder. "The manager is over there, the tall lady with the reddish hair; she can help you," she said.

James grabbed his license and balance slip and made his way across the room to plead his hopeless case. Having been in prison, he was quite versed in disappointment and heartache but this almost made him physically ill. Almost everything was gone, and although Linda was stunningly beautiful, James was suddenly disgusted with everything and everyone who had anything to do with his missing inheritance. "Do you have a minute for me?" he asked.

"Sure, Linda Stevenson; I'm the manager, and you are?"

"James Walters. My sister opened an account for me in this bank with you a little over a year ago," he said a bit more aggressively than intended. "I had almost eighteen grand in here up until the IRS levied the account in December according to Clare over there."

"Oh ... Oh, I remember your sister; you were in ... I mean ..."

"Yeah, prison. Don't worry, I didn't rob a bank. I don't work for the IRS," he said, the edge off of his voice now.

"I'm sorry, I didn't mean ..."

"No worries, I understand; none of this is your fault. I'm just ... pissed; not at you, but ..."

"I understand," she said. "I can give you a number to call at the IRS," she offered.

"I'm sure they'll see the error of their ways and give me my money back," James said, dripping sarcasm. "Sure, go ahead," he added.

"Wait just a minute and I'll get it."

He just nodded. He was against the ropes emotionally, but he knew he had to hold it together at least until he could get outside. His mind was racing; should he close out the account and take the cash? How would he rent a building? How would he live? *Hold on, cowboy*, he said to himself. *There's some cash in there. You'll make it. God is in control.* He tried to cheer himself up, but it was not taking root. He was mad, he was hurt, this was his mother's money they stole from him; it wasn't right. His mind was in a bad place right then and he was filled with rage and unimaginable thoughts that he tried to shake quickly. This was not a guy who needed much fuel for rage; a wounded outlaw is a very dangerous person. He struggled against insane thoughts, trying to reason with himself that these thoughts weren't his but that of the enemy; that this was spiritual warfare and God was in control and He wouldn't give him more than he could handle and all of that.

"Here's the number. I'm sorry this happened to you, hopefully they …"

"They are the IRS, Linda; they got me for something and that's how they roll," James said. "I appreciate your professionalism and your help, but I am not harboring any delusions about ever seeing that money," he added. "I'll be back in a day or so to open a checking account, but I better get out of here now. No offense, but I've had enough banking for one day."

Linda smiled at that, thinking she should be more nervous about this potentially volatile ex-convict, but something about him was calmly reassuring. Maybe it was his very green eyes. He wasn't a loose cannon, but she imagined that if he did explode it would not be pleasant. "Well, try and have a good day. You're riding, so it can't be all bad," she smiled.

He smiled back, appreciating the courage it took for her to make that comment. "Good point," he said and walked away shaking his head.

Chapter Nine

The sun felt good on his face as he exited the bank. He was still reeling from the realization that most of the money his mother had left him had been unceremoniously extracted from his account by an out-of-control central government. James was a patriot who had served four years in the United States Army back in the late seventies, which was a terrible time to serve. On the heels of an unpopular war for a largely ungrateful nation and a Commander in Chief who seemed more at home in front of a fireplace than inspiring the troops, morale was horrible and direction was nonexistent. A warrior needs purpose and James felt that his efforts were wasted and he rarely spoke of those years. A patriot with a deep distrust for government, he was at odds with much of the overspending, which in his opinion was a thinly veiled effort to create a dependency class that would ensure votes and weaken the nation. He'd seen nothing to sway his thinking another direction and much to further cement his own ideology. James was cynical and jaded and he trusted only a handful of people; this episode did nothing to modify his outlook. It was time to ride and think and pray, and not necessarily in that order.

Inside the bank, Linda watched as the rugged biker mounted his machine and sat with his head bowed, his hand resting at the bridge of his nose for a long minute, before he fired the ignition and buckled his chinstrap. He glanced in her direction but only saw his shining black and chrome reflection in the tinted bank windows, then eased out of the parking lot and exploded down the city street, accelerating through the amber signal light toward the freeway. He had no idea where he was going, his plans were dashed, he was alone and defeated and for a few minutes his life made no sense at all.

He screamed and yelled as long and loud as he could and headed west on the 10 freeway. This would be a very fast ride to the ocean. The music was by a Florida band named "Savatage" and its rage reflected his. He recalled a paper he wrote in college on the power of music and whether one's mood determined the type of music to which one listened or the music determined the mood. He couldn't remember the outcome and at the moment he did not care. He was tired of his own brain. He hated the way he thought, the constant banter between his ears. The loneliness and the fear was coming for him and he was ill prepared to fight. He just rode faster.

He tore through Fontana, Ontario, and Pomona and he rode like he wanted to die on the road that day. He took the ramp to the 57 Freeway too fast and felt the bike start to hop to the right as it struggled to hold its grip. James' mind raced as he rode through the panic, rear brake only, just a bit, downshift once, twice. He braced as the concrete wall came at him, shoulder debris now flying all around him; he could taste the dust and dirt, but the bike never hit the wall. He rode the shoulder, inertia still pulling him to the right, but as the high banking left turn straightened out, he managed to guide the big bike back onto the highway and like a sling shot came out of the turn unscathed. His blood felt cold and he began to cry, then broke down like a man at an untimely funeral. His tears splashed against the inside of his Ray Bans and he thought about pulling over, but continued down the highway yelling and crying for a couple of miles before he found his peace and it flooded over him like nothing he'd ever felt. The Bible speaks of a 'peace that passes all understanding' and James believed that the Lord had taken him through that valley of death in order to reach that place. A surreal peace filled him and everything was very quiet; even the normally loud and steady pulse of the exhaust sounded far off, his vision tunneled like he was looking through a telescope. A strange perspective manifested itself, like a video game he'd mastered that was coming at him in slow motion.

He rode like this for several minutes and found himself south of the 91 nearing the Big A, where the Angels played baseball. He thought about attending a game, then remembered it was January and laughed at his mental breakdown; then he laughed some more that he didn't care. Scripture was filling his head faster than he could think: *I will never leave you nor forsake you; I will be with you even unto the end of the age*, and he was glorifying God and thanking Him for his life, the same life he almost just ended in fit of selfish rage. His faith had failed him but the Lord was comforting him, not condemning him, like the Lord knew who and what He was dealing with. James remembered telling Marc the night before that nothing takes God by surprise and he knew right then that God was with him. God had kept the bike from going over the concrete wall to a certain death on the highway almost a hundred feet below.

James decided to pull over at the next exit and grab a cold drink and collect his wits, or what remained. He ran south as the 57 freeway became Interstate 5 and took the first exit, pulling into the first gas station he saw. After topping off his fuel tank he parked in the shade provided by a twenty foot high willow tree. He thought it was the greatest gas station tree he'd ever seen and laughed to himself for noticing the darn thing. He walked to the store and bought an iced tea and a bag of smokehouse almonds instead of the cookies he was eyeing. *Good move*, he thought.

The familiar rumble of several Harley Davidson motorcycles was getting louder as he walked to his bike. He turned his head to watch seven bikes roar up to the pumps, two abreast, with one last bike opting out on

119

the fuel. He could tell this was an organized club but couldn't quite make out the patch and didn't want to appear too anxious to learn their identity. Whoever they were they sure joked a lot, a noticeable departure from the focused intensity of the DMC on a run. There were some good times for sure, some great long weekend runs, but these guys were enjoying themselves and it was the middle of a weekday. James found himself watching their antics and realized how he missed the camaraderie of the MC. He hadn't enjoyed much freedom yet, but already realized that he was very alone. He had resigned himself to that life, at least for a time, especially since his parole conditions prohibited any affiliation with the only people with whom he'd associated in the past several years.

James noticed that two of the bikers were walking toward him, so he stood up from his picnic to deal with whatever was coming his way. His arm unconsciously moved toward his chest only to realize that the old familiar "cut" was at a clubhouse in Yucaipa along with his knife and Remington model 1911 pistol. This would be interesting. The guys looked menacing as hell.

"How you doin, bro? Kit, Prophets MC Mother Chapter," the gruff voice matched his white beard and barrel chest.

James chose to remain anonymous as far as his club affiliation; "James," was all he said as he answered Kit's extended hand with his own. The other Prophet was Tio, a quiet Sergeant at Arms who just observed everything around him. Kit was the chapter president and Tio had his back. James could tell the guy was measuring everything; it was his job. Nice enough guy, just quiet. Kit was affable and talkative. He asked James all of the normal questions, complimented his bike, and then informed James that the Prophets was a Christian club and invited James to attend a Bible study on Wednesday night at 7 p.m. In Colton of all places.

"Christians? You guys look like outlaws," James replied.

"Some of us were, bro. We left that world. Now we're outlaw Christians, I guess," Kit said laughing. The two men handed James their calling cards with their phone numbers and told him to call if he needed anything. James thanked them and indicated that he just might take them up on the Bible study.

"I could use one," he said.

Kit replied, "It's not a normal Bible study, bro. We have a big charcoal grill and eat like pigs, and then our chaplain gives us the word. It's pretty cool; you should come by." As the men talked, Tio yelled for the others to come over. One by one these 'outlaw Christians' introduced themselves to the stranger extending handshakes and laughs.

*These guys laugh all the time*, James said to himself. "You guys seem to enjoy what you're doing," he said.

Kit looked at him and said, "We get to serve the Lord and ride Harleys; what's not to enjoy?" and he laughed a great loud laugh. James found himself laughing with them. Old habits die hard, so James, noticing that Kit had introduced himself as the Mother Chapter P, inquired about other chapters. "This chapter and a Nomad chapter," Kit answered. "We have ... Gambino, how many patch holders do we have?"

The road captain replied, laughing, "twenty-eight, no, twenty-seven now.

"Yeah, twenty-seven," laughed Kit in what appeared to be an inside joke. "We don't worry about numbers, man; the power is in the message. Jesus only had twelve knuckleheads in his crew, bro, and they changed the world."

"Amen," said James.

Kit explained that they were on their way to scout a location for a homeless benefit run the Prophets were planning, and asked the chaplain to 'pray them out.' They formed a circle around James and each man held his hand on James' shoulders as the chaplain offered a prayer thanking the Lord for their new friend and requesting 'traveling mercies' be extended to them until they met again. The Prophets bid James farewell as they roared out of the gas station in a tight pack. By the sound of it, they had little regard for the speed limit. James liked them already.

Chapter Ten

Whether it was near death experience or the 'chance' meeting with seven of the only twenty-seven Prophets — small numbers for a motorcycle club, the DMC had over two hundred at last count — as Kit had mentioned, it's not the numbers, it's the power of the message with which they were entrusted. James fired his machine and after checking his watch, decided that he could indeed fit in a run to the beach for some lunch and still surf the rush hour traffic back to the I.E. He headed out to Interstate 5 south and rolled to Mission Viejo and then west to Laguna Beach. His earlier peace still with him, he quietly accepted his financial situation and determined that it could be much worse. He still had about twenty-eight hundred with the cash in his pocket and the depleted bank account. It occurred to him that being strapped in Southern California in January was decidedly better than it could be in other parts of the country.

He reminded himself that God was in control and if he was going to trust God for all things, he'd better start now. The laughter and brotherhood that the Prophets

MC had shared with him stayed with him. *Those guys are nuts*, he thought to himself, but the spirit of God was upon them and James saw it and felt it and thanked God for bringing them to him at just the right time. He marveled at God's grace. It was humbling but at the same time uplifting to think that God was that personal and that concerned about this battered servant to have orchestrated this meeting at just such a time.

The Santa Ana winds bring warm air down from the deserts and basically blow everything out to sea for a period of days several times during the fall and winter months. It makes for an absolute paradise at the beaches. It was breezy but nothing like the fifty-plus mile an hour winds out in Ontario and Fontana. James parked across the street from the Montage resort, and as he had so many times in the past, walked down the long stairs bordered by perfectly manicured landscaping framing spectacular one hundred eighty degree views of the ocean below and outstretched, seemingly forever. He ventured through the park where a man and his pre-school aged daughter were happily attempting to fly her kite. James watched them as he walked, almost falling victim to the melancholy thoughts of what might have been had his wife survived her fight with the cancer. James heard his phone ringing in his pocket. "Yeah," he answered.

"Yeah? Very professional. Hey, how come you gave my wife your phone number and not me?" Marc barked.

"Because I like her better than you," James responded.

"Good choice," Marc laughed. "So where you want to eat tonight?

"Wherever, bro; I don't care," James said.

"I figured. Okay, well, since I have to do all of the thinking in this relationship, how 'bout the Olive Garden off Hospitality? We ate there before with ..." Marc's voice trailed off.

"Yeah, I remember. I'll see you there at six if that works for you," James responded, ignoring the reference to an evening a dozen years ago when the four of them met for dinner.

"Yeah, six is fine; we'll see you," Marc said.

James caught himself. "Hey, bro, Michelle always talked about that dinner with you guys; she loved it."

"Yeah, man, we did, too. I gotta get back to work. Have a good one ... oh ... and you're staying at our place again tonight. Don't give me any of your crap! Goodbye."

James just stared at his phone and pushed the red button. *Freaking Marc*, he thought with a smile. He resumed his journey down the cement stairs to the small, semi-private beach that was nothing like the huge public beach a couple of miles north. James loved the spot; he had met Michelle at the Costco in Mission Viejo and tricked her into coming to that spot for a "picnic" one summer day many years ago, and they had spent many evenings there dreaming and planning their life together.

He smiled to himself while his eyes filled with tears. *What is it with today and crying?* he thought. *Jeez, enough already*; he shook his head to instantly clear all memories of sorrow. He stood there a few minutes talking to the sea as if God lived there. He determined right there to follow Christ as a disciple and not just a believer. He had reasoned that there was indeed a difference between the two and as he was an extremist in most areas he thought he'd better be "all in" for the Lord or not at all. Nodding his head as if to say, *all right then,* he began the long trek up the stairway that led to the street some two hundred feet above the beach.

He was going to count the stairs on the way back — a typical OCD thing for him to do, but he lost count — a typical ADD thing for him to do. *You are as screwed up as a football bat*, he said to himself. It was a good five minute walk up dozens of stairs and his legs were burning as he took the final forty or so at a brisk pace, two at a time. Thirty-four minutes still remained in the parking meter, but there wasn't anything he wanted to do that would fall within that time limit and being out of change, he determined to leave it for the next guy. It was always fun to find a meter full of time. *You're such a good guy. Weird, but good,* he thought. He decided to check the oil level in the bike so he rummaged through the hard bags for a rag. There was always a nasty cheap red shop rag wadded up at the bottom of one of those bags. He wondered how many years this one had been there as he pulled it out and shook it like it was emerging from the dryer. *It's always good for one more oil check*, he thought. The fluid level was perfect and the oil color was pure honey gold. That was a good sign. Back to the bottom of the hard bag went the rag and on went the helmet and sunglasses.

It had to be close to seventy-five degrees, middle of freaking January and the weather was insane. No clouds, just sun. "Thank you, Jesus," he whispered. He blew off lunch; the almonds carried him that far, they could get him to the In-N-Out in Orange off the 55 freeway at Lincoln. James figured he knew the location of most, if not all of the Southern California In-N-Outs. Pretty handy information, he figured. James headed north on Pacific Coast Highway determined to take in a few more sights and roll out to the 5 freeway and then take the 55 freeway split north. It was still early enough to avoid most of the traffic. He hated the Southern California traffic.

He considered the 241 toll road, as that was just plain autobahn race track all the way to the 91 freeway. That thought made him smile. It had been too long since he'd been on the 241 and that day it was calling him. He would forego the burger this time; there would be others. Nine minutes later he made the transition to the toll road and just as he remembered, nobody was on it. He brought the bike to one hundred miles an hour and set it there for the seventeen miles through the canyons to the 91 freeway. Only one toll sensor to evade and that was accomplished by centering the bike directly on the lane paint while passing under and between the lane sensors. Those things are set up to notice cars directly underneath them, a hundred mile an hour motorcycle on the white line between the sensors is invisible. He smiled. He figured that was probably not the smartest thing to do but then again a guy had to have some adventure in his life. *Grow up*, he said to himself. He figured at a hundred miles an hour he was covering a mile every thirty-six seconds. Then he thought that he must enjoy speed more than the ride or he'd ride slower. He was really getting sick of his mind. It just wouldn't leave him alone.

*That's it*, James thought. *That's why I stayed loaded all the time,* he surmised while setting the bike for a long arc of a right turn and then through its reflection to the left. The riding out there was spectacular, regardless of the mental gymnastics going on. *I used booze and drugs not as a departure from reality as my wife suggested, but as a departure from the insanity in my head.* James was exhilarated to have reached this epiphany, but almost as quickly decided that it was now useless information. *Would have been better to know this a few years ago*, he laughed.

He backed the bike down to ninety as he began the two mile long grade down to the valley floor and the awaiting 91 freeway. A contrast if ever there was one. The 91 is busy at three a.m., it's nightmarish during the day, and rush hour is anguish for the participants. There is a toll lane on the 91, but there's only one entrance back before the bend just east of Kraemer/Glassell Boulevard and if you miss that one you're toast. Unless ... yes, unless you make it to the far left lane and look for the opening in the yellow vertical plastic sticks which at fifteen mph or less will allow a motorcycle a clumsy merge onto the pricey toll lane.

There are several spots that will allow this maneuver without almost stopping; one just has to be aware and capitalize as traffic continues in spite of the biker's quest for entrance. Something sinister happens to otherwise rational commuters when they smell a rat. A rat who might be attempting to gain an advantage over other motorists as they all vie for pole position in the nightly death race. There are many tales of motorcycle versus automobile and the far more entertaining biker versus businessman-with-an-attitude conflicts. Bikers always have the last laugh as they roar away from the boot printed driver's side mirror.

James recalled a time many years before when a guy in a nice Porsche 911 cut off one of his buddies on a Florida exit ramp. After a heated exchange and several nonverbal hand signals, the driver rolled up his windows and hit his door locks and continued to verbally assault the biker. Evidently the guy in the car had forgotten to close his sunroof. The confrontation ended badly for him.

Chapter Eleven

Suffice it to say, James found the opening and straddled yet another painted line, confounded another sensor and while acknowledging his transgression, was unwilling to repent, as his twisted reasoning involved his payments of hundreds of dollars of fines over the years. Basically, he rationalized his crime. He resolved to work on this recurring pattern of criminal behavior in light of his pending date with his parole officer and all. Also, he was pretty sure his Christian walk could use some work in that respect. Funny, he thought, some things are easy to get past and leave behind but other character defects proved more stubborn. He'd have to give this some further thought. White lining traffic at freeway speeds was exhilarating but tiresome. The brain has to function like a NASA computer as stimulus rages against the rider.

James rode through Corona, continued east on the 91 through Riverside, and exited by the Harley dealer, as there was an In-N-Out burger joint at the bottom of the off ramp. After another delicious meal he laughed that it had been two whole days of freedom and he'd had two number one's already. He would have to taper off soon, but it was fun! As he pulled back onto the street he noticed an old Ford pickup truck parked at the Home Depot with a For Sale sign in the front windshield. James had an affinity for 1970s vintage pickup trucks and curiosity got the better of him. He wheeled the big bike across the street and pulled next to the two-tone brown and beige Ford Ranger. The truck was in good shape and the sign said, 1976 Ford Pickup 188,000 original miles, 460 V8 $1,000.'

Years before James would buy and sell two or three vehicles every month and make some good money doing it, too. Depending on the vehicle, sales could be fast and profitable. This truck could easily sell for fifteen hundred or more with some cosmetic assistance. The vinyl bench seat had excessive wear and several rips, but it appeared structurally sound. James pulled his cell phone from his jeans and dialed the number.

An older man by the name of Arthur answered the phone and yelled some answers to several questions. "Yeah, it runs good; why wouldn't it run good?" Arthur barked into the phone.

James liked this guy; he'd always had patience for the elderly. He figured they had paid their dues and he was taught to honor folks older than he was. Good training. "Well, Arthur, I'd be willing to give you say ... three hundred dollars cash and the rest in about two hours," James offered. "You want me to drive over there for three hundred dollars?"

Arthur yelled. "I want a thousand; don't try to rob me, young fella," he said.

"No, sir; I just want you to have a deposit so you know I'm serious," James explained.

"You say you want to buy it in two hours, then come back in two hours with the money. I ain't gonna sell it to nobody else in two hours; jeez, oh Pete."

"Okay, Arthur, I'm serious. I'll be calling you in two hours or less," James laughed and hung up the phone.

This guy was a piece of work. It would be worth it just to meet Arthur. James decided to find a closer bank than Colton, despite the pretty manager. Out of prison for two days and he was already putting thirty percent of his net worth on the line on an old truck. He'd taken risks like this most of his adult life. James used to say he'd rather do a deal than work a job and maybe that's what pulled him into the outlaw world. Guys were dealing everything: cars, boats, bikes, houses, some things legal, and some not so much. A guy could make a living doing deals. You just had to be aware of your surroundings and have a grasp on market prices on a variety of items. He once made two hundred dollars in twenty minutes buying and selling a large stainless steel shop sink he saw in the trash in front of a recently remodeled house. James loved a deal and he was pretty sure he could invest in some seat covers and some tire black and make a few hundred on this truck in a day or so. Cash, too; the IRS had enough of his money, they'd see none of this deal.

The nearest Bank of America was about five miles away and James was determined to have the money to Arthur in thirty minutes, not two hours. *I've got to get one of those ATM cards and a checking account if I am going to be a big shot business guy*, he thought. *This takes too much time*. With five hundred and forty-three dollars still in his pocket, he withdrew six hundred, figuring that a hundred and forty-three would be plenty for the night's dinner, if he was able to pick up the tab.

James called Arthur from the bank's parking lot. The elder seemed confused; it hadn't been two hours and why did he say two hours if he didn't mean two hours. James did his best to convince the old guy that he meant no harm, the darn bank was just faster than usual. "You know how banks are, Arthur; you just never know how long they will keep you," which seemed to satisfy the inquisition. They agreed to meet in fifteen minutes; yes, James was sure about the fifteen minutes.

"Don't say fifteen if you mean thirty, or thirty if you mean fifteen," Arthur lectured.

"Yes sir, I'll see you at the truck," James said to Arthur, who had already hung up the phone.

The old fella's charm was wearing thin, but James was a man on a mission. That truck meant a week's pay if he could flip it in a hurry. He called Robin and asked her to list the truck on craigslist for eighteen hundred with James' phone number. She agreed and indicated that she and Marc were looking forward to dinner. James told her a little about Arthur and told her that he'd be there for dinner if he didn't kill Arthur. Robin was silent.

"I'm kidding!" James yelled.

She laughed, nervously and then added that her friend Yvonne was looking forward to seeing him again. James was silent as he racked his brain for any memory of an 'Yvonne,' until Robin rescued him. "You know, Yvonne the dancer?" she asked.

"Oh man, yeah, Yvonne; how could I forget ... is she still dancing?" he asked.

"No, she's like the manager of the place, 'The Lamp,' I think is the name of it over in Rialto."

"Ah, the gentleman's club," he laughed. "You know, even when I was hanging out in those places I didn't think of myself, or anyone else in there as a gentleman," he said and they both laughed. "Well, tell her I said hi. She's pretty funny, too wild for me, gorgeous, too, but no thanks."

"Did I just hear my James say a girl is, 'too wild for me?'" she asked, giggling.

"Yeah, you did; see you later, doll."

"Yvonne always thought you were hot," Robin added.

"Goodbye, Robin," James said.

James blasted out of the parking lot, suddenly nervous that he might arrive after Arthur and didn't want to incur the old man's wrath. He thought it was pretty funy that after all he'd been through with the DMC lifestyle he was scared of a little old man. "Thank God!" James said out loud as he arrived at the old Ford with no visible evidence of the ancient seller. James checked his phone; it had been nine minutes. "Whew," he said. Amazingly, six minutes later a late 1980s Ford pickup truck moved slowly through the Home Depot parking lot and came to a stop two spaces to the right of the subject vehicle. Out of central casting he saw as Arthur swung his skinny eighty-year-old legs from the truck and all five foot six inches of him, sporting a new pair of khaki-colored Dickies overalls and weathered work boots, made his way toward the biker.

"You're early," the old man said.

"Traffic was better than I thought," James said.

"You don't worry 'bout traffic on that motorsickle, do ya?" Arthur said with a mischievous smile.

James beamed back at him, "Not too much," and they shared a laugh, which broke the ice. They chatted about the truck for a couple of minutes, something you have to do regardless of the level of interest. Arthur was the original owner and didn't need it anymore as he had a "new" truck. James loved that the twenty-eight-year-old truck was the new truck and couldn't wait to take the "old" truck home. James was already dealing with the 'I don't know if I want to sell it' disease that had plagued him for years. His before-prison collection of motorcycles and cars, which he planned to sell, had swelled to seven — four bikes and three old BMW's — he was partial to German engineering. Had it not been for the extensive legal bills, he would still have them stored somewhere but they were all sold in a period of two weeks, three years ago.

James was quite capable of re-stocking. He knew that he'd have to sell this one to generate some working capital but once he got back on his feet, he'd no doubt start piling up the vehicles again. It was a sickness he had inherited from his father. James remembered when he was about six-years-old and his dad had to trade in the Corvair in favor of a 1965 Mustang convertible. It was a ritual, his dad told James, to say goodbye to the little Chevy, as it had been a good car. His dad took James by the hand and placed their hands on the rear deck of the old car and patted her and said goodbye. These things tend to stick with a guy.

Arthur turned the key and the truck fired up without hesitation. James was amazed at the sound of the engine and even more so when he lifted the hood and peered into a time capsule. The engine and the firewall and fenders were showroom clean and it was then that James knew his earlier plan to offer eight hundred would be insulting and simply wrong. "It looks great, Arthur; sounds real nice, too. I'll take it." James attempted to keep the excitement out of his voice. "I'm gonna have to leave it here for a few hours while I get a ride out here, but you and I can work this deal right now. I've got your asking price."

"Okay, then, I have the title," the old guy said, rummaging through the old Ford's glove compartment. The registration is paid up till June so you ain't gotta worry about that, and you don't have to smog these old trucks either, so that's good, though this one would probably pass smog," he laughed. "These trucks are better than the new ones. I hate the new ones; they're all plastic. You know there's more metal on this truck than ten of these plastic pieces of junk on the road now," Arthur exclaimed, a bit agitated.

"I hear ya," James said, not all that surprised at Arthur's outburst. He had known a few Arthurs over the years. Time has passed them by, but they hold fast to their opinions, right or wrong. James peeled off six one hundred dollar bills and counted out the remaining from a wad of twenties and tens in his pocket and handed the pile of money to Arthur who, as James expected, re-counted every last dollar. James laughed to himself about how this would have gone had James offered less than the asking price. He imagined that Arthur would have either lectured him on negotiation techniques and how they didn't apply to him or he would have cussed him out and jumped into the 'new' truck and drove off without selling it to him.

"It's all here," said Arthur.

"Well, good; you didn't leave me with much," James said with a smile.

"That ain't my problem," the old man said, matter of fact. He was a character, this guy, but James was enamored with the man.

"I'll take care of her," James said, and immediately felt like a lying dog as his immediate intention was to sell it and make a few hundred dollars.

"Don't matter to me, it's yours now," Arthur said unconvincingly. The old guy turned and ambled to his truck. He did take one long look at the Ford before he slowly drove away.

"You old softy," James whispered.

Since he was sitting in front of a Home Depot, James figured this would be a great opportunity to replace the home made cardboard 'for sale' sign with a nice new one. The smell of a Home Depot took him back several years. Memories of his and Michelle's remodel projects. There were three of them. He smiled to himself as he relived 'the greatest hits' compilation in his mind. Funny how you only remember the good times; all the arguments and damaged feelings pale in comparison to the overall blessings received from working on projects of purpose. He missed her sense of humor and obsessive nature when immersed in the project of the month. James used to shudder at the word as he knew it would involve his back and his wallet. The old adage rang true: 'You don't know what you have until it's gone.' He shook the memories from his head. *Only you could take a trip to Home Depot and turn it into a chick flick,* he realized. *Big, bad biker crying in the lumber aisle. Clean up in aisle eight. Bring a mop; biker crying,* he continued. *Focus dude; knock it off.* After wandering through the entire store, James settled on a big fat Mr. Sharpie and a shiny new red and white 'For Sale' sign with separate spaces for information, price, and phone number. *Fancy*, he thought.

~

James stepped back a few feet and admired his work: '1976 Ford, 188K miles, runs great $1,800.' He wrote the phone number and placed the sign back on the dash with a small piece of tape salvaged from Arthur's old sign. James laughed to himself as he imagined Arthur's reaction if he happened upon the truck later today. James strapped on his helmet, slid his sunglasses into place and rolled out toward Moreno Valley. He figured he had an hour or so to check out a few warehouses and make some calls. His plans changed in light of his altered financial situation, but overall the goal remained the same. Find a fifteen hundred square foot warehouse with a small office in front. A roll-up door was essential as there would be motorcycles in and out of the place. Instead of a separate apartment, he would frame up some sleeping quarters, or if possible, convert an existing office. He would purchase an airbed, a microwave oven, and a used refrigerator. A gym membership would provide a hot shower and a daily workout for about thirty bucks a month, which was cheaper than a water bill. He smiled at his Spartan plan. It was elegant in its simplicity. James loved efficiency. His only wish was that it wasn't always born of stress, but then again if a person has the means, these measures, though quaint, are usually unnecessary.

James rode toward San Bernardino, which would have hundreds of suitable locations. It was a great spot for a shop, as the area hosts thousands of motorcycles with plenty of riders who want more speed. James was a master at getting the most from a Harley engine. He was banking on the fact that most riders would rather pay a guy to 'trick out' the bike than to do it themselves.

Chapter Twelve

James exited the freeway at Anderson and headed north to a group of industrial buildings, several of which could serve his purposes. As he rolled north on Tippecanoe Road he noticed a small storefront next to several dilapidated old Craftsman-style bungalows. He imagined how quaint this street must have been seventy-five years ago before the strip malls and sprawling shopping centers crept in. These little structures were like stubborn boulders against the crashing sea, still standing as the flood waters of progress surrounded them.

James admired them and slowed the bike to take a longer look. He spotted a man on a ladder next to the free standing storefront. The building was only thirty feet or so wide but extended deep into the sliver of property that backed up to another street by way of a crumbled asphalt driveway. The building's position on the street looked like an afterthought, such was its odd placement, like it was inserted. After backing the bike against the curb, James placed his helmet on the seat and walked toward the ladder.

"Are you a realtor?" the man asked. He had a rechargeable drill in his hand and was attaching a rain gutter to the side of the fascia.

"Do I look like a realtor?" James answered, his tone a bit short. He laughed as he realized he probably sounded overly gruff.

"Just gotta check; they've been after me to sell and I'm not interested," replied the man.

*Another Arthur.* "I'm just looking around for a building to rent and I saw you working here, so I figured maybe you could give me the lowdown of the area," James reasoned.

"The area ain't so nice. You got the money across the street, but the neighborhood is still the same over here," said the man as he climbed down from the ladder.

James extended his hand. "James," he said.

"Bud," said the man as he shook James' hand, still holding the cordless drill.

"This your building?" James asked.

"Yup, one of my vast real estate holdings," Bud laughed.

"More than most people have, 'specially these days," James said. "I like this place; it doesn't look like all the other cookie cutter buildings 'round town. You planning to rent it?" asked James.

"Eventually; it needs a bit of work before I can do that," Bud said.

"What if a guy wanted to help you fix it up; would you extend some rent credit in exchange?" James asked.

"Depends. I guess; what you got in mind?"

"Well, I need a place to work on some motorcycles and I'd be very willing to work around the place for a couple months' rent and if we can agree on a rent after that, I'd be interested in staying for at least a couple of years, maybe more," said James, surprised at what was flowing from his mind to his mouth.

"So you just roll up on your bike and make me an offer like that; you on a mission or something? You know like the Blues Brothers — you on a mission from God?" Bud laughed.

"I like to think so," James answered. "Today's been kinda like that for me. I just may be on a mission from God."

"Well, James, I sure didn't expect you today, but I'll think about your idea."

"What's to think about, Bud? I need a place, I'm willing to work, you ain't gonna rent it for a couple months anyway. What do you say, you've got nothing to lose."

"Man, you are crazy, you know?" Bud said.

"Oh, you're not the first person to make that observation, brother," James laughed.

Bud said, "I don't know why I'm doing this, I might be the crazy one here, but you got yourself a deal ... I think," he laughed. "You're a bit nuts, but like you say, I don't lose much if you flake out on me. Here's what I'm willing to do. You help me fix this up, I'll let you have the keys, you get two months no rent. I gotta get nine hundred a month after that. You can rent it as long as you want; we can do a two-year lease to start. I'll supply the tools and materials; whaddya think?"

"Can I look around inside first?" James answered.

"Oh, sure, you got me thinking so much I forgot you haven't even seen inside. You may change your mind!" he laughed.

"I doubt it," James said. "I've got a feeling about this place."

Bud handed James several keys on a key ring with a faded yellow rubber 'Inland Plumbing' advertisement printed on it. "These are the spare keys; you'll need 'em to get in and out when I'm not around," he said. "Now I've got to get rolling; I'm going to Victorville to look at a pickup truck. I need a beater truck to haul stuff. I have another project a couple miles from here, worse than this one," he joked.

James laughed out loud. "What kind of truck you looking for?"

"Nothing much, maybe two grand. You know, just something to haul stuff from Home Depot and Lowe's; they love me at those places," he said.

"Well, what if I told you I know where you can buy an old Ford long bed in great shape for eighteen hundred bucks and you won't have to drive to Victorville?"

Bud answered, "If it's in any kind of shape and it runs, I'd say I'll take it."

"You can follow me; it's up on the 91 at Indiana in the Home Depot parking lot. You can test its hauling capabilities!" James laughed.

"I know right where that Home Depot is. I can meet you there in thirty minutes; no need to try to follow you on that thing," Bud said as he tossed his head toward the motorcycle. "My 'bug won't keep up with you," he added.

James felt that familiar tug at his spirit and offered to ride with Bud in the old Volkswagen as there would be a logistical challenge getting the truck and the 'bug back to San Bernardino.

"You can put your bike in the building, just roll around back and I'll open the big door."

As James rode around the short block that led to the back driveway of his new headquarters, it dawned on him that he had not seen anything of the inside, save what he could make out through the dusty front windows. He was never big on details but this was crazy even for his standards, loose as they were. *I'm stepping out in faith*, he said to himself and to the Lord. James figured that if the spirit of the Lord was indeed living in him then silent prayer and worship must certainly be heard by an omniscient God. James knew that this was the place that God had for him; things were too smooth and so far from the regular method of operation that this had to be God.

James glanced at his phone as he climbed into the vintage Volkswagen. He figured he was good for another hour and a half before he was to meet his friends for dinner. He considered a quick visit to a department store or a Walmart as the black t-shirt he'd been wearing for two days was nearing its limits of viability, at least for a social gathering. *Some outlaw*, he thought. There were times when a good t-shirt and jeans would last a week or more on a run. This might be disgusting to a normal citizen, but to a biker it is business as usual. Style and hygiene are not priorities. James had always prided himself on looking and smelling as nice as possible, but after a few years with the DMC, his focus shifted to survival and conquest. It was a terrifyingly different world and it was going to be difficult to assimilate back into society.

On some levels prison life was more civilized than the previous seven years as an outlaw. Folsom served up three meals a day and a guy could generally enjoy eight hours of sleep, and never at a rest area in the rain. The state furnished television, newspapers, and in James' case, an opportunity to study Bible curriculum for two and a half years to become an ordained and licensed pastor. Prisoners are a captive audience in many respects. James took full advantage of much that was offered to better his life and pass the time, not always in that order.

"Gotta stop at the ATM on the way just in case this truck is worth buying," Bud said with a smile.

"No problem here. I'm not on much of a schedule these days," James answered.

The drive to the Home Depot was uneventful as it was difficult to carry on a conversation in the little bug. "I love these cars," James said. "They are as dependable as the weather in Southern California." he added.

"Yeah, it ain't much to look at, but it runs good," Bud replied.

"I'm glad you're partial to function over style, Bud; the truck ain't much to look at either, but it runs great," James laughed.

Bud was silent for a couple seconds, then laughed and shook his head. "I should have known."

The men drove on in as much as the small talk as the little old car would allow. Every bump, though capably managed by the car's suspension, announced itself audibly.

The bigger pot holes were much more challenging. Bud's hands were both on the wheel, which liberally moved from side to side as the car ricocheted from bump to bump. James enjoyed every minute of the ride. The excitement of the past couple of hours was building in his spirit. He was careful not to assume too much regarding the pending transaction, but all things considered, it was going well. It was obvious to James that God was in the middle of this entire orchestra from the abyss that was the morning bank visit and nearly catastrophic ride through Pomona. Meeting the Prophets, buying a truck, finding a building, and possibly selling the truck, all by 4 p.m. It was an amazing run.

Bud stopped at a bank a couple of exits shy of their destination. "They're open; you mind waiting here while I run in?"

"Not at all. I'll see if I can sell this thing while you're gone," James joked.

"Better not," Bud chided. "I'll make you walk to the truck and drive it to me!"

"Touché," James laughed. He really liked this guy and recanted his earlier judgment; he was no Arthur. Bud was probably late fifties to Arthur's eighty-plus and Bud seemed to have a demeanor about him that didn't ruffle easily. James gravitated to people like him.

Bud was back outside in a flash, which prompted James to ask jokingly, "That was fast; did you use a gun?"

Bud just winked at him and said, "Let's get out of here," and they both laughed as Bud attempted reverse several times before finding success.

"Remind me to choose a different getaway car next time," Bud said laughing.

"If you can't find 'em, grind 'em," James answered. He imagined that he and Bud could enjoy a friendship as much as a landlord and tenant could be friends. As his daddy would have said, Bud was 'good people.' James was determined to see this through and help Bud with his 'project' building regardless of how long the lease relationship lasted. He was taught to leave things in better condition than he found them.

James had no reason not to think the Ford would still be sitting where he left it, but it was still a relief when they turned the corner and the truck was obediently in place. Bud parked the bug in the same spot Arthur had occupied earlier. The men silently walked to the front of the pickup truck. James admired his 'For Sale' sign and lamented the seven dollars he'd spent if this guy did indeed buy it. He handed Bud the keys and turned his hand as if to say, 'it's all yours.' The truck behaved perfectly in spite of its new owner's betrayal. James was already feeling like a lowdown rotten human being for selling the truck after telling Arthur he'd take good care of her. Thirty-two years with the same owner and then within two hours to be traded like a minor league rookie baseball card was beneath this truck's dignity. James shook his head to chase those thoughts away. *It's a stinkin' truck, for crying out loud*, he told himself in an effort to quell the guilt. *This is all your fault, Pops*, he said to his deceased father's memory. "It's a stinking truck." he whispered. Bud popped the hood and listened to the hum of the big V8. It sounded fantastic and truth be told it would have sold if it ran poorly, such was the condition of the engine and compartment. "Pretty clean, huh?" James said.

"I'll say; how long you had this thing?" Bud asked.

"Not long," James answered. That much was true. "I bought it thinking I would need it, but I need the money more than I thought," James added as if more words would somehow mitigate the fact that he'd only owned the truck for less than two hours. "I bought it today, Bud. I got a decent deal and thought I'd flip the thing and make a few bucks." There, he said it. That wasn't so bad, was it? James felt the weight of the world fall from his shoulders.

Whatever was happening to him was happening fast and he had no idea why he couldn't flip a simple truck deal without confessing the sins of his childhood before a perfect stranger who had no call to ask him anything!

"No kidding; today?" Bud asked. "Well, son, if you make any money at eighteen hundred, you deserve it; I'll take it. I was gonna drive forty-five minutes up the hill and deal with some two thousand dollar imported piece of junk that probably couldn't hold a candle to this one." Bud reached into his pocket and pulled out a wad of hundred dollar bills and carefully counted eighteen of them and handed them to a stunned but very happy James Walters. "You got the title or is the ink still wet?" Bud laughed at his own joke.

James was thrilled but managed to calmly pull the folded pink slip from his wallet and hand it to the eager new owner. James smiled because he never even filled in the new owner's portion of the document. It was ready to transfer from Arthur to Bud. James was a ghost. James had not even thought past the deal, how they would get both vehicles back to San Bernardino.

Bud looked at James and asked if he'd like to drive the pickup back to the shop for him. He said 'sure' and jumped in the truck he had so nonchalantly discarded. He was determined to explain to the truck what had happened and that it wasn't the truck's fault; it was him and the truck would be better off without him. Bud would take better care of her and they could still be friends as they would see each other often. He was insane, pure and simple, but it was a conversation that he had all the way to San Bernardino.

James arrived at the building a couple of minutes before Bud, enough time to park the truck and make his way to the front door and coerce the slightly bent and considerably worn door key to convince the lock to surrender one more time. James was sure this was just one of those key-lock relationships that needed to be understood by the key master. They worked together just fine as long as the key was pulled back ever so slightly before turning counter clockwise. It was a feel, not a measurement, and once that was mastered, entry was a breeze and no re-keying or new locks would be needed. One only needed to agree to the terms, getting by without shoving, as it were. A new and gentler philosophy for James but one to which he was amenable. After all, he owed it to the truck.

Once the lock was negotiated, the door opened gingerly exactly half way and then either the floor rose to meet the door or the door was hung at a slight angle but the result was stoppage, halfway, and an almost broken nose for James, who had followed the door a bit too closely. "Whoa," James exclaimed as he stopped just short of needing gauze tubes. "I'll have to get to this right away," he said out loud to no one.

Bud pulled up and noticed his new tenant's run-in with the door. "That door sticks a bit," he yelled to James with a big smile.

"Noticed that," was the reply. "I'll get it taken care of in the morning, my first order of business," James added. "Mind if I look around real quick?" he asked.

"It's yours now; be my guest," Bud answered.

"I'll be back early tomorrow to get a start on some stuff; you gonna be around?" James asked.

"Not tomorrow, I've got some business to tend to this weekend, but I'll be here Monday if you need anything. Here's my number in the meantime if you have any questions," Bud said, handing James a business card that read simply 'Harold "Bud" Parker, Investor.' A cell phone number rounded out the printed information.

"Fancy card," James joked.

"It does the job," Bud replied. "I'm going to leave the 'bug here tonight. I think I'll give the truck some love if I get some time, gimme a chance to get to know how she acts," Bud said as he extended his hand. "It was good to meet you, James. I'm sure I'll see you soon."

"Likewise, Bud; thanks for the opportunity. You won't be sorry. I'll fix this place up." James replied. Bud turned and walked to his new old Ford truck, climbed in, and started the engine. James spoke above the engine noise, "God bless you, Bud Parker; thanks again." Bud looked at James for a long moment and then nodded his head and waved as he pulled away.

James turned sideways and squeezed through the available space between the half opened front door and the door jamb. "I could keep it like this to make sure I don't get too fat," he mumbled as he flipped the two light switches and waited for the old school florescent shop lights to come to life. The place was empty and fairly clean. The greenish floor tiles screamed 1972, while the ceilings spoke late fifties with their nine foot height and ornate crown molding. The walls were in need of paint. Large picture windows on either side of the front door would yield — with some soapy water — voyeuristic views through industrial strength bars of a moderately busy street and dozens of businesses recently planted across the street as far as you could see in both directions. 2012 was in full swing on the west side of Tippecanoe Road, while the east side was fully fifty years behind. James liked his side of the street much better. He would enjoy frequenting the variety of eateries and shops, especially coffee shops, but he would much prefer a 'to go' order eaten in a busy motorcycle shop than to share a meal with the attitudes on the west side. He had no clue, no inkling whatsoever, as he stared out that dusty window that in due time they would come to him.

## Chapter Thirteen

Outside of the outlaw world, the only two people he didn't want mad at him were meeting him at the Olive Garden in exactly one hour. James headed out the front door, then carefully locked it behind him. Time would allow a quick visit to the nearest Walmart and as he was equidistant from two of the massive stores, he chose the Washington exit location. As this was the first visit to the retail behemoth in three years he was surprised to be greeted by a produce department and, oh by the way, an entire grocery store somehow now fit inside the already colossal store. *Brilliant*, he thought.

Things were noticeably more desperate than he remembered. There had always been folks asking for spare change, but it seemed now to have become a cottage industry. No less than three people asked him for money from his parked motorcycle to the front doors. He tried not to be judgmental, but it seemed to him that all of these people were young and quite able-bodied, so he just walked past each of them ignoring their loud requests.

As convenient and efficient as a Walmart store could be, James never wanted to stay in one for very long. The noise and incivility of many shoppers depressed him, especially around Christmas, his favorite holiday. Thankfully, and this sounds very strange, but thankfully, he had been in prison the month before and hadn't had to face the shoppers selfishness and greed that was replacing community and goodwill. He had witnessed society's deterioration over the years but it was more evident in his recent return to 'civilization' and it was depressing. James moved with purpose through the men's department and the health and beauty aisles before allowing himself a foray into automotive. He was curious to compare the price of oil and filters and such items three years removed. He was sure things were much higher but couldn't remember any specifics. He settled into the knowledge that we pay whatever they tell us to pay or we don't buy it.

His attention was drawn to a young mother with a little boy at her side and an unidentified infant in a covered stroller. The woman was pleading with the counter person, a man in his twenties, to please just repair the flat tire and put the best of the four on the front. The young man was explaining that none of her tires were salvageable and her purchase of just one new tire would be unsafe. James could tell by her tears and her mannerisms that this was an unexpected nightmare and he figured it probably could not have come at a worse time. He imagined there would never be a good time for this. The two had obviously come to some understanding as evidenced by the clerk's shoulder shrug and the woman's child caravan moving to the customer waiting area.

James approached the counter and asked what kind of car the woman was driving.

"It's an old Toyota, man; her tires are tore up," the young man, tag name of Greg, explained.

"A Toyota. What's the wheel size? Can't be more than thirteens," James replied.

"Yeah, thirteens. She's buying one tire and I'm telling her that it's not safe, you know?" Greg pleaded.

"Yeah, well she obviously hasn't budgeted for this so here's what you do, bro: ring up the other three tires right now and I'll pay for them, valve stems and FET and all the B.S. that goes with them — mounted, balanced, whatever — just do it but don't tell her. Just get the tires on her car and that's that. You dig?" James asked.

"Well, yeah; is she a friend of yours?" he asked, a bit taken back by the strange biker taking over his department.

"Does she freaking look like a friend of mine? I don't know her, bro, but she's cool; she's taking care of business with those kids, so let's just take care of this, okay?" James said.

"Yeah, okay; no problem," Greg said. "The tires are on sale for forty-three eighty-eight plus the …"

"Yeah, I know. Plus, plus, plus; whatever, bro, just tell me what I owe you," James said, more nervous than upset. He just wanted this to end so he could escape.

"What am I supposed to tell her? She's gonna ask what this is all about," Greg asked.

"Tell her that Jesus loves her; can you do that for me, bro?" James was smiling now.

"Yeah, sure; yeah, I can do that ... you really don't know her, do you?" he asked again.

"You're catching on, Greg; you'll be store manager in no time, bro." James reached over the counter and gave the guy a good-natured pat on the shoulder.

Greg began entering the transaction details in the register when he asked, "Can I get your name and address?"

James laughed and said, "Make something up, bro," and quickly peeled off two one hundred dollar bills. "Can I buy this stuff, too?" he pointed to the shirt and assorted HBA items.

"Sure, let me get those for you." He slid them over the electronic eye on the counter. "One eighty-eight seventy-seven is the total for everything," he said as James handed him the money. "Mister, that was one cool thing you just did," Greg said with wonder in his voice.

"Praise the Lord, brother." James replied. "See ya 'round, Greg."

Once outside, James tore into the packaged black dress shirt like a five-year-old on Christmas morning. He was careful to capture all of the forming cardboard and plastic and deposit those unnecessary items into the outdoor trash can through the filthy hinged opening. "How hard would it be to Pine-Sol these things once in awhile?" James wondered. This was another strange observation for an outlaw biker.

He returned his attention to locating and removing the half dozen or so pins strategically located throughout the new shirt. Satisfied that he had eliminated the risk of random skin puncture, he shook the shirt and unbuttoned the 'never needs ironing' garment and looked it up and down before removing his t-shirt and donning the stylish replacement. The fleeting thought that most people resisted the temptation to get dressed in a Walmart parking lot was quickly brushed aside. *Economy of motion*, he thought. James wadded up the t-shirt in the plastic bag that contained assorted toiletries from his Walmart visit and dropped it into the left side hard bag. On went the helmet and shades and out of the parking lot went the Inland Empire's best dressed biker.

After the high speed slalom course on the 215 north to the 10 east, James backed her down to take the Waterman Road exit, which meant the Olive Garden restaurant was less than sixty seconds away. As usual, James was early. He'd operated on 'Lombardi time' since he learned the concept from his high school football coach. Coach Phil would always say, "If you're early, you won't be ... late!" The whole team had that speech down and whenever he said it, he always put the delay between 'won't be and late' so the team could yell 'LATE' in unison. It was corny but highly effective. Every former player James ran into over the years would say it and laugh. A young man could learn much from a good coach. James had coaching football on his bucket list' and maybe some day he would offer his services as an assistant at a school ... but who would hire an ex-con as a football coach. He shook that thought from his head, no use thinking of things that could never happen.

Chapter Fourteen

James parked his bike in front of the building under some disapproving looks from two young couples who were entering the restaurant. He was used to those looks, although it had been a few years since he'd experienced them. Anything that breaks the continuity of the norm was looked upon with suspicion and disdain. People were creatures of habit and there was nothing like an outlaw to upset the applecart of the daily routine. James had never sought trouble but had always been quick to call others on their judgmental behavior. He hated the haughty and arrogant nature of people and enjoyed shaking up the perceived balance of things. After quickly determining that the couples were posers who thought they were special with their pricey Lexus SUV and fancy clothes, he thought they should be enjoying their dinner at a five-star restaurant and leave the Olive Gardens to the common folk. 'Big fish in a little pond,' his father would have said.

James had no sooner finished sizing them up than he felt the all too familiar tug at his spirit. *I love them as much as I love you, James,* the almost audible voice said. *You're judging them as they judged you or like you thought they were judging you,* it continued. *Oh, wow, busted again*, he thought with a laugh. *You can run but you cannot hide*, the loving assault continued. "Okay, I got it," he said out loud. Having a relationship with the living Christ could be quite interesting. It was like having an inside joke with an imaginary friend, only this friend rules the universe and is the Alpha and the Omega of all matter, and oh, he's not imaginary; he's more real than that motorcycle parked out front.

James was excited not only to see his friends and hopefully continue their conversation, but that God himself, in the manifestation of His Holy Spirit was quite literally present and accounted for tonight. James knew he was not alone and that this divine appointment was set up quite possibly several thousand, or million years ago and it would be kept! How cool was that, he thought. James' job was to show up and he had done that, new shirt and all.

As he was a few minutes early, James approached the hostess and took the liberty of requesting a table for three under the name Walters. Then he spotted the archway leading to the men's room and thought to ensure his dapper appearance extended to his 'helmet hair.' Exiting and blocking the entrance to the men's room was one of the party of four who had treated him earlier with 'that look' outside. James resisted the urge to crush the guy's knee and smash his face into the Samuel Adams mirror that graced the wall opposite the door. Instead, possessing a discipline the likes of which he'd never experienced, James excused himself and stepped aside while the guy moved past. *Now that's growth, bro*, he commended himself. *You're going to be quite a finished project someday*, he smiled.

The thought crossed his mind that God was able to create galaxies, solar systems, and all manner of life in six days, yet *he* was going to be a project. That level of arrogance would require further examination. Free will must be a bigger obstacle to progress than anything known to mankind. James remembered something he'd read in the gospels where Jesus was telling one of the Pharisees that their traditions would make what Jesus was teaching of no avail. Traditions and free will or man's stiff-necked rebellion were no doubt responsible for all non-progress in the history of the world.

This epiphany was interrupted by the unshaven, unkempt face staring him in the men's room mirror. James started laughing, *No wonder those people looked at you like you belong in a zoo; you look like an animal.* He did the best he could with some water and soap, but only managed to moisten and straighten out the knots in his hair. He was glad he chose a black shirt as the rain falling from his head was mostly invisible when it reached his shirt. He lifted an arm and wiped his hair straight back with his sleeve. *Amazing*, he thought. *Let's go see if these nice people will even serve you tonight.*

From his vantage point in the hallway, James noticed Marc and Robin enter the foyer and move toward the hostess podium. James came up behind them and made eye contact with the hostess as he put a forefinger to his lips. She smiled at him as he made his move.

"Mr. Walters has been waiting for you. Please take a seat in the bar while your table is being prepared," James said in his best maître d' impersonation.

"Well, how good of Mr. Walters to think to have us wait at the bar," Marc laughed in his loud Midwest voice.

"You two look great," James said.

"You look like crap!" Marc replied.

"Marc! Stop it, please. Oh, my gosh, James, I can't believe him. You look nice; is that a new shirt?" Robin asked, shaking her head like it was the first time her husband had ever insulted anyone.

James had already put his arm around his friend's neck in a mock headlock and said, "I expect and will accept nothing less from this guy," he answered as they approached the long mahogany bar. The bartender was a beautiful dark-haired woman who stood eye to eye with James' six foot tall frame. His gaze never left hers as she asked what his friends were having.

"White wine," Robin answered.

"Vodka grapefruit, hold the grapefruit." Marc loudly laughed at his old joke.

James and the bartender enjoyed a long moment as James ordered a club soda with a lime.

"My pleasure; pull up a seat," Kathleen replied.

James turned to his friends and motioned to the nearest table.

"You don't want to sit here," Marc whispered as he moved his eyes toward the bartender. "All bartenders are treacherous, bro, and the pretty ones are the worst."

I'd just as soon sit over here," James said with a big smile. "I'm getting too old for all of it," he added. "Besides, after twenty minutes she's gonna figure out I don't have any money or a job and my most recent mailing address was Folsom, California," which caused the three of them to bust up laughing just like the old days.

Marc continued, "That would have never stopped you before; in fact, it would have been even more of a challenge."

"Yeah, but now I'd just want to preach to her, " James laughed.

"Oh, no, please not the hot bartender ministry!" Robin chimed in, which just extended the laughter.

"Sign me up!" James said.

Kathleen waved to James to indicate that his drinks were ready. He jumped up from the table and took three steps and met her at the bar. "What do I owe you?" he asked.

"$12.50. I can run you a tab if you want to take those to dinner," she replied with a wink.

"Nah, you don't want me owing you anything. I'm liable to run out on you," he teased. It seemed old habits die hard and he always loved to banter.

"You have honest eyes," she said.

"Maybe, but the rest of me is pure outlaw," he laughed and handed her a twenty with a wave of the hand indicating they were even.

"Well, thank you!" she said.

"The pleasure was mine," he said, turning back to the table and to his two friends staring at him with big smiles.

Robin slowly shook her head. "You're incorrigible."

"What? How could you say such a thing?" James feigned his pain. "I'm just being nice. She has a hard job and probably works all night for a lousy forty bucks in tips. There's no bar business here," he said with an experienced tone.

"Ah, well, that is noble of you," Robin said.

"He's a giver," Marc added.

"It's who I am," James said slowly. They all laughed. "I missed you guys." As he raised his glass of club soda and joined the others, he added, "To friends and freedom!"

"Here, here," Marc said, slamming his vodka in one pull.

"Oh, no; it's not gonna be one of those nights, is it?" James asked with a grin.

"Nah ... well ... maybe!" Marc laughed. "I had one of those day and I needed that," he said.

"It's trucking, bro; it's always one of those days!" James added.

"Yeah, but back then, back when we worked together with that old crew, it wasn't like it is now," Marc lamented.

"Yeah, we had fun, that's for sure." James turned to Robin. "We were insane but we did an awesome job; the competition between us, what did we have, like ten of us?" James asked.

"Thaddeus, Kelly, Derek, Johnny Shoe, Jeff, Kevin, Mike, Bob, the 'Blade!' Marc recalled the crew.

"The Blade! Man, whatever happened to that crazy mother?" James asked.

"No clue, bro; he's gone off in the desert to howl with his relatives!" Marc laughed.

"As crazy as I got, the Blade was always a step crazier and he lived to be the craziest; he made it his business to be nuts." James shook his head. "Dude, you know I never ride on the back of anyone's bike. Me and him got all twisted up one afternoon and the next thing I know I'm holdin on to the Blade like I'm his girlfriend and we're doin wheelies on the 10 through Colton runnin through the gears and he gets that thing up to one-thirty-five with me on the back! Do you remember that bike? It had a freaking wheelie bar on it to keep it from flipping backwards! I am so done with that brand of lunacy, man. I couldn't keep up anymore if I wanted to. Nothing's left for me out there," he said.

"What about the club?" Marc asked. "They're gonna respect the terms of your parole, but you know they will come a knockin the minute you're clear."

"I know, I've thought about it a little but I have a year to get something going. We'll just see what happens, what the Lord has in store," James said, happy that he was able to publicly give it to the Lord. He would pitch a strong game that night and take any and all opportunities to defer to God and give Him the glory. The awkwardness of the other night was long gone, the old friends were back in the groove, and James would use that time to hone his skills as an apologist for the Christian faith. He never liked that term, but that was the proper description. Marc had indicated that there were some questions he'd like to discuss and that was an opening James was going to enter. This was not some multi-level business venture; this was a man's eternal soul, salvation, an issue much bigger than life and death.

James just laughed to himself when he saw that the hostess had seated his party of three next to the table of four. It seemed the Lord had some unfinished business with his judgmental attitude. The guy from the bathroom hallway scowled at James, who pulled his chair and positioned himself so as not to look at the four adjacent dinner guests. Marc and Robin were oblivious to the animosity developing between the tables and James was determined not to add any fuel to the situation by allowing himself any eye contact. He was a new creation in Christ, but he was still just a man, a man who was very accustomed to terrorizing the general population, albeit generally with a crew.

It is safe to say that normal people have not engaged in countless all-out brawls. The guy in the cubicle next to yours is most likely not a veteran of dozens of bar fights. He probably would not look at a room quite like an outlaw biker looks at a room. James surveyed his surroundings like a frightened animal. He routinely sat with his back to the wall and his eyes to the front door. He parked his motorcycle such that an easy straight path to the exit was always available. If, God forbid, he ever drove a car, it was always backed into the parking space. With Marc seated across from him, James knew his back was safe, and with James, Marc never worried about his own.

James had already inventoried the table; half carafe with fresh flowers would make a dandy club, forks and knives were a given, and a quickly broken plate would complete his makeshift arsenal. *Only a violent and crazy person would qualify weapons at a dinner table,* he realized. He wouldn't give it another thought. his work here was done and the information filed away for the unthinkable. Better to be prepared. "I'm pretty hungry," James said.

"What else is new?" asked Robin. The server was a college freshman named Evan who was studying

Political Science at nearby Cal State San Bernardino. James resisted dismantling his young, idealistic, liberal viewpoints and determined to 'play nice,' much to his dinner companions' relief.

"You have mellowed," Marc observed.

Thinking about his earlier plans for the broken dinner plate, James chuckled, "Yeah, I'm a regular pacifist now, bro.

"And you think that's because of Jesus?" Marc replied intently.

James searched for the sarcasm that ordinarily accompanied most anything Marc said, but found only the focused look of a man in search of peace. "Yes, I do." James said. "I know the 'me' before Christ and the 'me' after Christ and there is a marked difference," James continued. "It's not just some prison conversion, bro; I know I have the spirit of the risen Christ living through me and there is a peace, which the Bible calls, 'The peace that passes all understanding,' that I now have and it's incredible and I wish it for everyone."

"Wow," Robin said softly. "I just got chills."

"It's the air conditioning," Marc laughed. They all laughed. "Sorry, we're gonna be loud tonight!" Marc said to the table behind James. "I think we're disturbing their meal," Marc said. "Too bad," he added. Marc was the greatest friend and husband, but he made a lousy enemy. His Chicago upbringing and his U.S.M.C. background, 'once a Marine, always a Marine,' made him —as James would describe him — 'loud and proud.' On many past occasions James was actually the voice of reason and that was terrifying as his fuse, though long, could burn quickly. Marc, on the other hand, seemed to have only two speeds, neutral and wide open! A few short years ago the two of them could trash an entire restaurant, drink their beer, and steal their women.

Robin was a female version of Marc and James found himself silently hoping that the people behind him would resist any inclination toward confrontation tonight as there was important spiritual business to conduct. It had occurred to him that the enemy Satan would attempt to thwart this discussion and might very well use pride and arrogance as a spark. After all, it's worked for centuries.

James turned his chair slightly and leaned back, "We'll try to keep it down. We're just catching up on some lost years," he said to the group.

They all replied with versions of, 'no problem, 'don't worry about it,' and 'have fun,' as James returned his chair to its earlier position.

"In-ter-est-ing," Marc said.

James silently smiled at his friends. "It's all good," he said.

Dinner arrived and James moved his recently finished salad plate to the side. The food seemed to cover the whole table. Bread sticks, pasta, steaming piles of glorious Alfredo, the first 'sit down' meal in just over three years and it looked and smelled wonderful. James stretched one hand out to Robin and his other over the table to Marc and said a quick prayer of thanks for his friends and the bounty of food before them. He asked for God's will for their lives and in the name of Jesus Christ, they all said "amen."

James savored the first delicious bite of his Chicken Picata for what seemed like ten minutes. It was so enjoyable he actually closed his eyes while chewing. A bit dramatic, but this was an unexpectedly more wonderful meal than he'd imagined. Prison food evidently took its toll on his taste buds and this dish was awakening them. As with most things in life, we don't know how good we have it until they're gone. In this case, he'd grown so accustomed to the salty, preserved gruel in prison that this middle-grade restaurant food was magnificent. James made a mental note to maintain this level of thankfulness.

"So tell me again why Christianity is the only way to God?" Marc asked, seemingly out of nowhere.

"Geez, honey, give the guy a chance to enjoy his dinner," Robin interjected with a laugh.

"No worries," James said. "I'm happy that he wants to know. I can eat and preach," he laughed. "Well, here's what I've determined, brother, and it's really cemented my faith. God's holiness can't abide sin. It's totally incompatible; it cannot coexist. This is pretty huge when you get to the exclusivity of Christ question so remember this part later. God, in His infinite love for mankind gave us free will which, if you think about it, was an unbelievably risky thing to do. Not risky for God because His existence and future is totally independent of ours, but risky if you want this perfect, no-problem relationship with your creation."

James finished his water and asked the passing waiter to fill everyone's drinks as, 'this might take awhile.' "So here He is giving his creation total access to Him, amazing surroundings in Eden, they could want for nothing at all. The only thing He told them to stay away from was the tree of life. Ever see a wet paint sign and want to check? Yeah, well, it turns out that these two knuckleheads just couldn't leave well enough alone and they, not just Eve, bro, *they* deliberately disobeyed God, with some help from the devil who, true to form, lied to them about the consequences of this disobedience. He said, 'If you eat this, you will be like God' and in direct contradiction to what God told them, 'you surely won't die.' Dig this, the Bible says he told Eve but it also says that Adam was with her, meaning he was standing right there and he knew better but he was willing to disobey God just to make this chick happy. Sorry, Robin, but that is what happened. Adam should have manned up and said, 'Are you nuts, beat it; we aren't falling for the banana in the tailpipe trick,' but he just stood there and allowed it all to happen," he said with a smile. "Check it out; when God confronted Adam, the dude blamed God by saying, 'it was the woman you gave me who screwed up.' This guy was classic!"

There was a bit of laughter with this explanation but his two friends were listening attentively and James found himself speaking so fast that he felt electric, like he was plugged into the wall. He took another long pull from his ice water and continued. "So with this rebellion, sin entered into the world. Now this is massive, as you will see down the line. This sin nature is what we've all inherited and it's exactly why Jesus had to enter into the world and deal with the sin issue, which absolutely explains why only Jesus could deal with this. But I'm getting ahead of myself here; I want to hit on that later because it explains so much."

"Proceed, counselor," Marc chuckled.

James ignored him and continued. "So back to holiness and why Christianity is the only way to God. The holiness issue is why, when people think they can be good enough to get to heaven on their own, it's ridiculous. God's holiness is inconceivable in its totality and magnificence. It's not just good or great or beyond anything we can understand. Moses was a great guy called by God, and all he wanted was to see God's glory. God basically told the dude that he'd blow up if he saw it. He didn't know what he was asking, but he begged God to see something. God gave him a millisecond glimpse of the tail end of a shadow of His glory and Moses lit up like an aircraft landing light. His whole being was glowing in the dark from just a tail end view for half a second. That was God's glory! His holiness is in that glory; it can't be understood and that's why God can't allow sinful man to get anywhere near holiness. It can't happen. It's not that God won't let it happen, it *can't* happen. God's only remaining true to His essence by this law of exclusion. The fact that evil man would even think doing a few good things in his miserable life would somehow override sin is so pathetic, so laughable once you grasp holiness, hearing such nonsense is maddening. We've inherited a sin nature; we aren't sinners because we sin — we sin because we're sinners." James stopped there for a drink as well as for effect.

Marc and Robin were wide-eyed and it was obvious to James that this was making sense, so he jumped right back before anything distracted his small audience. "This sin nature deal is important because it was the eyedropper of poison that rendered the whole bucket poisonous. Water molecules at the bottom of the bucket are just as poisonous as ones at the top, even though they didn't have initial contact with the poison. Adam and Eve screwed up, but you and I are heirs of that condition. Now before you go blaming and hating them, realize that if it were you guys instead, we'd still be in the same boat. If not them, someone would have messed up. We are incapable of living in obedience to God. Hence the law, which we'll get into at a later date. That is, if you'll eat with me again after tonight," he said with a chuckle, which lightened everyone up for a minute.

"This is huge, because I run into people all the time who think that they can't pray or go to church until they get 'cleaned up,' like their sin is just too much for God to handle. This is a lie from the pit of hell. Satan is hell-bent, if you'll pardon the pun, to keep people in this mindset. He's trying to tell us that we've gone too far. Who are we kidding thinking that we can go to church and try to foster a relationship with God; our past or present is too dark."

James paused to see if he'd lost them yet; so far so good. "As long as the devil can convince us that it's the sin we commit that keeps us from any hope of redemption, he's won. But God is saying that it's not what we do that keeps us from God, it's who we are, and who we are can be changed by entering into an agreement with Him that what Jesus Christ did at the cross was and is sufficient and nothing we do is remotely enough. Forgiveness is not just an event; it's a place!" He continued. "The Bible says 'anyone who is in Christ is a new creation; old things have passed away.'" James stopped as he saw Marc shake his head.

"Back up a minute," Marc said. "Forgiveness is not just an event, it's a place? What the heck are you talking about? Don't you ask forgiveness when you sin?"

James smiled and answered his friend. "Brother, you just asked a question that has kept me awake many nights, but I am so clear on this now. It is my life's work to preach this wonderful grace gift, but I warn you, this will crush any religious teaching or ideals you have built up. This is beautiful two-hundred-proof grace and it makes people crazy, either with joy or with rage and I dare say, it's what crucified our Lord. I hesitate to speak on it now, but then again I think it's the most important explanation of scripture in history. Jesus Christ took sin away. He defeated it completely and we are to rest in what He accomplished. We are to rest in Him and quit trying to add our pathetic manmade religion to what he said was finished."

James paused again and took a couple of bites of his now lukewarm dinner. He didn't mind much; even at room temperature this meal was better than anything he'd eaten for years.

"This is interesting, I'll give you that," Marc said.

"Given the participants, I'm amazed that we're having this conversation at all." Robin added, "You've got to admit it is pretty weird, the two of you having a civil discussion on biblical matters. I guess there really is a God," she laughed.

"We laugh but it's true, when you think about it. There was another guy inside from another MC I had the opportunity to minister to for several weeks and after all of the scriptures and archeological evidence, the thing that brought him to a saving knowledge and acceptance of Christ was the fact that a slime ball like me could go from a raging psycho, fighting every day, to a guy filled with peace." James added. "It's called a witness, basically how we act after we've come to Jesus Christ, and it's not our doing. That's another big hurdle. People always think and say it's us that's changed, but it's the power of the Holy Spirit in us that is performing the work; we are just along for the ride if we yield our selfish nature to Him."

"Okay, I still don't see how this is any different than any other religion," Marc argued.

"That's my fault," James said. "I'm going too fast and forgetting your initial question. Let's back up a minute. Without going into a long Old Testament study here, suffice it to say that God required the priests to offer sacrifices to cover the people's sins. This was a covering, not a permanent deal, as it only took care of the sins to date. Basically, every year they offered the blood of bulls and goats and such because God required blood for the remission of sins. This is important, too, and we'll get back to it. The people, being sinful losers like we all are, started giving God their less than perfect animals for sacrifices. Like if we were required to give one of our animals, even though God required our best offering, we gave him the old tore up goat instead of the young strong one. They didn't trust God, either; nothing has changed on that front. God saw this, of course. He doesn't miss anything and because He knew before the formation of the world that all of this was going to happen, He had also prepared the perfect sacrifice for our sin. The Bible says that 'he who knew no sin became sin,' and that is Jesus Christ, the perfect son of God. Instead of just covering sin with imperfect animal sacrifices, God offered the one sinless, blameless, perfect sacrifice for sin. In several places, the Bible says that this offering was 'once for all,' which means exactly what it says. Once for all sin and once for all sinners!" James paused for more food and some water.

"No other religion has God coming to us to offer a solution for the disease we all have, which is sin. All the other religions have a series of do's and don't's and what to wear and what day to show up and what to eat. It's all manmade; it's us trying to reach God in some abstract, nonsensical plan. Christianity is God reaching for us; all other religions are man trying to reach God. You dig? All others are works-oriented religion and Christianity is grace-oriented," he said.

"Makes sense, I guess ..." Marc replied.

"The more I study it, the more perfect I see that this plan is," James added. "All religions accept that Jesus was a man who did and said wonderful things, some will even allow that he performed miracles, but Jesus was not just a great teacher or prophet, He claimed to be equal to God. No other religious figure in history claimed that. Not Buddha, not Mohammed, not anyone.

Jesus Christ is part of the Holy Trinity of the Godhead which includes God the Father, God the Son, and God the Holy Spirit. God loved us so much that He came here and offered himself as a sacrifice once and for all for the sin of the world."

James stopped and leaned back in his chair. "That's why they killed him," he said emphatically. "No one had a problem with Jesus being a great teacher and prophet; they had and still have a problem when He claimed to be God."

"I see your point," Marc replied. Robin was slowly nodding her head as well.

"Check it out. If Jesus was a great man, a great teacher, one to be revered and respected and He claimed to be God and He wasn't God, would he be a great man? Or a charlatan, a liar, and anything but a great man. He didn't leave that option available for us; he's either God or he's a madman. Deal with that my friends," James said, tossing his white linen napkin onto the table.

"Excuse me, I'm so sorry to interrupt," came the voice from the adjacent table. "We just heard what you said and I have one question," she asked.

"I'm sorry if I was loud," James said. "What's your question?"

"Are you a preacher?" she asked. "And where's your church, because we want to go!" and with that, everyone laughed. James just smiled and looked at his two friends who were smiling right back at him.

"Sounds like someone's plans are going to change," Robin said.

"We'll see," James replied. "I'm glad liked what you heard," he answered. "There is no church, just a desire to preach the gospel to anyone who will listen," he said.

"Well, you should have a voice. You should preach the way you just did to your friends because that will reach people," came the male voice. The guy who James had earlier determined would end up with a fork in his neck was standing over him with an outstretched hand. "I'm Derek. This is Tim and Ella and Bria," he said, shaking James' hand. They were from the area and each of them had written their names and phone numbers on Tim's business card and handed it to James.

"In case you ever start that church, we will support you," Ella told him.

James introduced himself and his friends to the group. He was grateful for the encouragement but couldn't help thinking he was cut short. There was so much more to say, but it was not something you could cover in one night anyway, so maybe this was just as well. He would get with Marc and Robin again; they'd been friends for years and the odds were pretty good that this would be taken up again another time.

"Why don't we all get together and have dinner?" Bria asked.

"That would be great," Robin answered politely.

"No, I mean like Sunday night at our place. We have a big patio and we could have a bar-b-que and, well, if James wouldn't mind, maybe we could review and take this further? I, for one, have more questions," she asked with slightly raised eyebrows.

James looked at his friends for a way out but none was available. They looked at him and Marc said, "It's up to you, preacher man."

"Fine then, give us the address and we'll be there." James answered before he could escape.

In a game in which the two of them had always engaged, Marc was able to gain the advantage during the handshaking and exchanging of phone numbers and negotiate the dinner check from the waiter without his friend's notice. Marc was noticeably victorious as James actually looked like a man who had been conned and had just realized his exposure.

"How did you ...? I was in perfect position for the waiter's approach! I had you ... ah, the confusion between the tables gave you the opportunity, you slick dog," James said with admiration.

"You guys are unbelievable. Anyone else would be happy if someone picked up the tab, but you idiots feel like you got worked if you don't have to pay!" Robin said in mock disbelief.

The two men laughed and raised their water glasses to each other in a moment of mutual admiration. They had, over the years, manipulated the dinner check from each other using ever more diabolical means that would make any secret agent envious. This was just a classic distraction and if James didn't know any better, he might suspect his friend had set up the whole adjacent table in advance just to 'win' at dinner. Weird dudes, these two.

James walked with his friends into the cool night air, which had noticeably chilled in the two hours spent inside. "Looks like the Santa Anas are dying off; it's getting cold out," James noted. Like a sailor, a biker pays attention to the weather and James was always aware of subtle changes that could make his preferred mode of travel more of a challenge than usual.

"Yeah, it's actually supposed to rain a bit tomorrow but clear Sunday midday," Robin said. "You're staying with us tonight, I hope," she added.

"Yeah, I appreciate it. I got a place today, kind of a fixer but I like it. I'll tell you about it when I catch you at the house later," James replied. "I had a great time with you guys. I hope I didn't get too preachy, but …"

"No, not at all," Marc interrupted. "That was good stuff, bro; I've been thinking a lot about what you said and it makes sense," he admitted.

"Thinking about it while you were scamming the check more like," James pointed out.

"Well, I did take a minute to work my magic," Marc laughed, slapping James on the shoulder. "One thing, though; how does the forgiveness work in relation to salvation?"

"I'm glad I'm not the only one who wanted to ask that," Robin added.

"Good question, bro. Here's where you enter into the covenant and it's not a big mystery. You don't have to call a priest; just talk to the Lord, tell him you know you're a sinner, and you need a savior and that he's the only one who fits that bill and thank him for taking your sins to the cross. Ask him to fill you with his spirit for eternity. It's something you can do on your way home, bro; just do it. He knows your heart. In fact, let's do it now; seriously, it's the most important decision you can ever make."

"Okay, I can't believe this, but yeah, I'm ready," Marc said.

"Me, too; I want to be sure," Robin said.

"Pray with me then. Heavenly Father, thank you for sending your son to take our sin; we admit we are sinners and we need Jesus. Please fill us with your Holy Spirit and abide in us for all eternity. We rejoice today that we are entering your kingdom Lord. Amen."

"Amen," the two said in unison.

"Praise the Lord," James added. "The Bible says we are now joint heirs with Christ. This is awesome!" James hugged his two friends.

"I'll see you later; you know the way," Marc said.

"Be careful, honey," Robin said, kissing James on the cheek.

"Yeah, you, too; see ya later," he turned and headed to his bike.

When he reached the bike he noticed it was already soaked with dew, a telltale sign that cold and moisture were invading. James headed back inside to load up on paper towels from the men's room, as his oily rags would do nothing but spread the water all over his seat and there was no worse feeling than a cold, soggy seat, no matter how short the ride. In a slight detour of reasoning, he decided that an absorbent bar towel would be a better solution, so he made his way back to the raven-haired bartender to negotiate a piece of dry terrycloth.

Kathleen was washing glasses from the tail end of a late rush when she looked up and caught his gaze. "Well, hello. I thought you were long gone," she purred.

"Not yet; we ate and talked too much tonight," he answered. "I'd like a dry bar towel if you can spare it. My bike seat is soaked and I'd rather not sit on it if I can help it. I'll bring it back. They just do a much better job than the men's room paper," he laughed."

"You can keep it for now," she said as she pulled the towel from the belt of her black slacks. "Maybe you can bring it back another time. I work every Friday and Saturday night," she winked.

"I'll do that; thank you. Have a great evening," he said, turned to walk away.

"You, too. Don't forget, Friday and Saturdays," she said, emphasing the *and*.

She was incredibly pretty and James was excited that she had shown that much interest, but what was he going to do with her — invite her over to the new place? That would do it. *Here's a paint brush, baby; how YOU doin'?* he laughed to himself. There would be time for romance again someday, but for the immediate future he needed to concentrate on making some money and furnishing a modest roof over his head. He could invite her over to Marc and Robin's, but then they'd have to contend with the wolf in the back yard and the snake and the other dozen or so rescued animals. Nope, stick with the plan and trust God for the right woman and the right timing. He'd had enough of doing things the James way. She was pretty, though.

As James was finishing up wiping any trace of moisture from the seat, gas tank and mirrors, he took the liberty of wringing the towel out onto the asphalt and wiping off the effects of the day's ride from the front fairing and windshield. His new friends were noisily exiting the restaurant when James kiddingly said, "Hey, can you keep the noise down over there?"

This out-of-character outburst was greeted with laughter and good-natured bantering. "See you Sunday, Preacher; don't forget."

To which he replied, "I'll be there. You guys take it easy out there tonight. It's Friday, lots of amateurs out there."

James sat on his bike for a couple of minutes reflecting on the evening. The four people he had misjudged earlier had become friends, Marc and Robin were responsive to his unpolished presentation of the gospel, and the pretty bartender was hitting on him. Oh, and the food was really good. Not a bad night and all things considered, not a bad day; he'd only lost about fourteen grand.

He fired up the big machine and let it idle for a minute. These air-cooled bikes ran like mad in the chilly night air. This would be a great night for a long ride, but he was feeling the effects of a long day and quite possibly the fifty years on his body and decided to call it an early night if his friends would let him rest. He reminded himself that he needed to rejoin the 24-Hour Fitness down the street from his new digs, maybe tomorrow. He loved the twenty-four hour part as he'd often worked on bikes late into the night and a good workout and a hot shower was a great way to end the day. He'd need a healthy alternative to the nightlife he knew with the DMC, that was for sure.

Chapter Fifteen

The first mile was colder than he thought it would be, which solidified his decision to get to the warm house. Somehow the cold seemed colder these days and the occasional thought of having another vehicle entered his mind. *Man, you are getting old*, James said to himself. *You just need some better cold weather gear.* He'd have to check the date on the next biker swap meet over in Long Beach; those were epic gatherings. A guy could get all the parts for anything he was building as well as top notch deer skin gloves, chaps, leathers, facemasks, everything he'd ever need for easily half of what a dealer would charge.

He would really need to look into a pickup truck of his own. That Ford would have been perfect but he really needed the money. He'd keep an eye out for another one. Thoughts of swap meets and parts runs and bike building were running through his mind as he took off from the light at Alessandro. That was when he first noticed all the lights up ahead. A sobering chill ran through him seeing the piercing blue and red flashing strobe lights of emergency vehicles up ahead in that familiar intersection. He saw three police cars and one ambulance already on the scene with a fire engine and second ambulance arriving as he slowed the bike and planned his route to avoid the mess if possible. Though he could not see the vehicles yet, James began to pray for whoever was involved in this one; it appeared to be pretty bad judging by the amount of emergency personnel already engaged. Traffic was now slowed almost to a stop and he was still a couple of hundred feet from the intersection. He inched forward, looking for a spot where he could split the lane and get through, but found himself submitting in a form of reverence to the obvious gravity of the situation. Someone's life or lives had been altered in a moment and the thought that it could happen to anyone was sobering, as it always is when life is so violently interrupted.

At first it looked like only one vehicle, but as James rolled closer he saw a second vehicle and actually felt his blood turn cold with dread. He could make out that silly 'who rescued who?' sticker on the back bumper, but the front of the van had disappeared into the front end of a lifted pickup truck. James ignored the police as he quickly pulled his bike behind an all too familiar Riverside County Sheriff's car and with one motion had the bike on its kickstand and his body halfway off the bike.

The noise of the 'jaws of life' sounded a block away as James ran, seemingly in quicksand, in the direction of the twisted metal. Two officers grabbed him as he ran to toward the carnage. Their voices joined the machinery in the distance. James fell to his knees about six feet from the van. He could see Marc's lifeless, smashed, bloody torso while the fire department worked in feverish symphony in a vain attempt to reach his old friend who, an hour ago, was cheerfully carving new memories. James tried to focus on the passenger seat, his eyes frantically searching for Robin. He saw a paramedic reaching through the windshield with bags or an oxygen mask — James couldn't make it out which. His knees started to throb; he must have landed on the pavement a bit hard but quickly dismissed his discomfort as his friends' bodies were crushed and bleeding to death in front of his eyes.

James heard his anguish in the cold night, his own distant voice screaming for Marc, desperate to reach him to somehow tell him that he was right here, that they were not alone. My God, my Christ! Oh no, no, no, please don't let this be happening. Robin! He screamed loudly and then surrendered to the suffering, his own sobbing center stage, the artificial lighting from the cars and the sweeping beam from a helicopter paralyzing him. He cried out for God but felt horribly alone and abandoned. My *God, my God, why hast thou forsaken me?* echoed in his spirit. He knew right there on the bloody street that God did not abandon him but that His word was hidden in his heart and that God was, even now, comforting James with his word, though the excruciating joy of that moment might never be shared with anyone for fear that it could never be adequately explained. The paramedics were defeated; their eyes betrayed them as they looked through James.

The firefighters dutifully continued to tear the minivan to pieces in a effort to free what remained of the occupants. Death was all around and it was palpable. Complete strangers were sobbing on the street corner, their pity-filled eyes watching James as he, with the help of two officers, staggered from the scene and slumped against the curb. "What about the animals?" James said to no one. "They'll have to open another shelter to fit 'em all," he laughed. He must have looked strange sitting on the curb giggling as his best friends lay mutilated in their van.

Random thoughts raced through his head as he sat on the cold curb. What should he do? Who would call their famiies? Who would call their friends? Who were their friends, even? They ran in different circles. Should he call Marc's employer? Should he ignore them? Marc hated that job anyway. James smiled to himself. He wouldn't call them; he owed Marc that one! James looked over at the rescue attempt, which began to look methodical. Gone was the urgency and the yelling of instructions. Surely his friends were dead. He managed to stand and as he did an officer took notice and walked toward him. "Do you know these people?" he asked.

"They are, were, good friends," he answered. "Are they dead? They look dead. Everything has slowed down. It doesn't matter anymore, does it? They're dead, aren't they?" his voiced tailed off.

"Yes, I'm very sorry." The officer seemed genuinely grieved. "If it's any consolation, I'm sure they were killed instantly."

"Not quite instantly," came a voice from behind the officer. "Sorry, I overheard you, and I'm really sorry, dude, but the man, he didn't die right away; the lady did, I'm sure. God, it's awful, I'm so sorry. I heard the man, what was his name, sir?" the young witness asked James.

"Marc," he replied.

"Well, I was there at the corner and when it happened I ran out. I was in shock, too, man; it was just so freaking horrific. I'm sorry, I'm sorry, it was just, I didn't know what to do! I called 911 as I'm sure others did, but after I hung up I yelled into the van and the man, Marc, I could hear him groaning and I got close and I heard him say something so scary; well, not scary, but like awesome or, oh, man, I don't know. I heard him say, "yes, Lord, yes Lord," two times and then I yelled to him and then I didn't hear anything else." His eyes were wide. "That was just ... I don't know, it was like some weird … I can't explain it," he sputtered.

"I can," James said softly. "He was entering into the presence of the Lord right in front of you, bro; a lot was going on right there. You might want to pay attention; the Lord was giving you a glimpse into His majesty and His mercy and maybe you need to pay attention. Did you think that it was just chance that you were here tonight?" he asked. "I don't think so. I can tell you that nothing happens by chance," my friend. You were supposed to see this and hear this tonight; it might not seem like it right now but this is an amazing blessing," James said with warmth and compassion as if it were this guy's friends who lay lifeless under two yellow tarps in some grisly sideshow on a damp city street.

"Wow. I don't know what to say," the guy replied.

"I know, bro, me either, except that Jesus is real and He must have quite a plan for your life. Thanks for sharing what my buddy said before he let go over there; he was a great dude. They both were great people and I will miss them, but I will be comforted knowing that they will be there when I get there," James said. "And you, what's your name, bro?" he asked.

"Randy," the guy said.

"Well, Randy, my name's James and I am a pastor and I would suggest that you … do you have a Bible?" he asked.

"No," Randy said with a nervous look.

"Hang on." James walked to his bike. He rummaged through the right side hard bag until his arm emerged with a small orange New Testament with Psalms and Proverbs that he'd received from some street minister years ago. James walked back to Randy and handed him the little book. "Now you do. I suggest you begin with John, Chapter One, and ask the Lord what He would have you do. You dig?" he asked.

Randy, not desirous of irritating this crazy biker over something like this, thanked him for the Bible and excused himself.

"You better read it; God might not miss you next time," James laughed.

He was laughing a bit too much, given the circumstances. He chalked it up to shock. "Yeah, I must be in shock," he said out loud. "Marc said, 'Yes, Lord' huh? Twice? Well, it's good that he didn't go arguing." Now he was laughing uncontrollably. "This probably looks bad," he said, but he couldn't stop laughing. *Who's going to feed the freaking wolf?* he thought.

James thought about riding over to the house to make sure nothing was there that could be incriminating for Marc, but then remembered that Marc was dead, so it wouldn't matter much. Still, there could be crazy stuff lying around that might fall into the wrong hands, like the cops. It was becoming more and more evident that James was incapable of rational thought right then. *James is insane right now; please leave a message,* he laughed more to himself.

Maybe the better diagnosis was manic — his mood shifts were all over the map. Deep joy can be experienced while laboring in sorrow and the depths of unhappiness. Sound strange? Sound impossible? Not really, because joy is a depth of soul, a knowledge that something, in this case salvation, is guaranteed regardless of current circumstances. James was struggling with the loss of his friends, but joyful that his friends were in the arms of almighty God in a place of such permanent beauty that the human mind is incapable of imagining. In light of this fact he rested in that joy, while on the other hand the human, 'I'm stuck in this lousy fallen world surrounded by pain and death and selfish, hateful people,' reality made for some unhappy thoughts, of which we all can relate!

Our hero had been out of prison for only three full days, ridden in a truck for eight hours, lost most of his dear mother's inheritance, almost crashed his motorcycle, bought and sold an old truck and taken possession of a rundown building in a questionable neighborhood, unable to contact or associate with any of his acquaintances per state mandate, and his only real friends were being removed from their minivan in pieces. It would be a lie to say that he was very happy right now. Joyful, sure, he knew that he was in Christ and the Bible says that makes him a new creation, and he was most certainly that. The fact that the drunk twenty-year-old who had erased the lives of his friends just minutes before was still alive in the back seat of a sheriff's car and hadn't been beaten to death by this grieving friend was proof. Gone was the hate-filled rage that would have dominated James' spirit a few short years ago, such that this young defendant would never have made it to the safety of that back seat. James even felt some pity for this post adolescent — not much mind you — but pity nonetheless, as his young life was irreparably damaged. James had even spent a minute or two pondering that lack of rage and desire for vengeance as the 'old' man was certainly still alive and not well in his spirit.

Thankfully, James was not aware that this most recent transgression represented the second DUI for the kid or his self-absorbed lack of remorse would have sent James into a tailspin, which could threaten everything good that God had meant for him. That being said, he did jot down the license number of the kid's truck; old habits die hard. James stood there for several minutes thinking, what exactly is the protocol for administering dead friends? Does he follow them to the hospital-slash-morgue? Does he continue to their house and spend the night as if nothing had happened? What about the dogs? He wanted to go over there and make sure they were fed but they'd eat him if he just walked into their home without their owners. This whole thing was crazy. He was crazy. James walked over to the nearest sheriff deputy. "Hey, I don't know what to do with this, but they live … lived … down the road about a mile and they have a grip of dogs and cats at their house that will need attention. I just thought you should be aware," he said.

"Yeah, we have people who will check it all out. Did you know them well?" he asked James.

"Very," he answered. "This is a bad night. It started out okay; we just ate a great dinner and were all headed over to their place, but this happened," he said. "Did that guy get hurt?" James asked, nodding over to the man handcuffed in the back seat of the car.

"No, he's fine, which is often the case," he said.

"Is he loaded?" James asked.

"Suspicion," was all the cop said.

"Yeah, sure." James huffed. "He'll get his," James mumbled and in the next breath added, "I'm outta here," and walked toward his motorcycle. He resisted the urge to turn and look one more time at the scene. He decided then that he would head back to San Bernardino and sleep at his building. He'd have to move in sometime, might as well be that night. He could not bear to spend the night at their house.

The bike roared to life and James slowly weaved in and out of the emergency vehicles, glancing at the crowds that had gathered at each corner. It was Friday night after all; everyone needed a show. The green light signaled his loud exit from this living hell. The icy air met him instantly and he enjoyed it like he needed to feel the discomfort to purge the darkness from his mind. His friends were dead and he was alone with the grief that surrounded his mind and served to further alienate him from the rest of the world. The enemy was working on him already, and as stealthily as ever. Everyone has a weak spot and for James, it was loneliness and mourning. He'd fallen hard after the deaths of his parents and his wife and this was a perfect time and place for another epic tailspin. James was breathing grief and abandonment right then. He stopped at Stater Brothers market and bought a couple of nice steaks to toss over the fence. The wolf would love them.

## Chapter Sixteen

He was awakened by the cold. The makeshift bedding of blue jeans and a wadded up drop cloth mitigated the hardness of the floor but offered little insulation. *Note to self, buy an airbed and a blanket.* He was getting too old for this. The sharp pain in his lower back could be minimized by curling into a quasi fetal position and allowing fatigue to ultimately declare victory, sending him into another hour or so of sleep before the cold and the pain came around again like a random CD in a six-disc player.

When morning finally arrived, it was everything his first morning at Marc and Robin's was not. It was not warm, it was not bright, there were no birds in this neighborhood, and nobody had programmed his favorite brand of hot coffee to meet him in the kitchen. If he had felt hope and strength the morning before, he felt fear and loneliness today. He knew to whom he could attribute this feeling of dread, and he knew he should be on his knees praying for guidance and strength to resist the enemy, but he just didn't feel like it that morning. There are times when a person actually enjoys pain; they wallow in it. His wife called it a 'pity party.' He really missed her right then. (Turns out even tough guys need love and understanding sometimes.)

He wanted a beer and a cigarette, but he neither drank nor smoked anymore and thankfully, there wasn't a liquor store next door. There was one down the road but he'd come out of the ether by the time he walked all that way in the cold and that was the end of that stupid idea. No, what he really needed was some eggs and coffee and a workout and a hot shower, the order of which didn't matter at all. He gathered his clothes and headed to the 24-Hour Fitness. With any luck he could sneak in and work out and shower without signing up and parting with any cash, at least until Monday.

It was only a three minute ride to the gym, but James was wide awake when he arrived. It was definitely winter again, so much for the Santa Ana winds. He'd have to wait another week or two for another helping of desert winds. James was convinced that the older he got the farther south he would have to move. He figured that by age seventy-five he'd be somewhere in Equatorial Guinea!

As luck would have it, a far too energetic fitness associate was at the front desk flanked on each side by brand new trainees! Praise the Lord! "Hi, welcome to 24-Hour Fitness," the high octave voices greeted him as he entered.

His first thought was to turn and run, but he'd made it this far and truth be told, he needed a shower. "Good morning," he grumbled, "I'm looking to join," as he reached for his wallet, a beaten man. He knew he was doomed with the trainees and the energy of the late teens descending on his hopelessly outmatched early morning countenance. James feebly attempted the free pass, but he soon realized that it would be infinitely less painful to just sign the darn forms and pay the money. It was embarrassing and he was glad he was alone that morning. God forbid any of his brothers, or anyone else for that matter, witnessed this pathetic exchange.

As he walked to the men's locker room he remembered that his best friends had been crushed to death the night before. *That really happened,* he thought.

After a decent run through a chest and triceps workout and a gloriously hot shower, the cloud was starting to lift. "Thank you, Jesus," he said as he slumped against the cold steel of the gym locker. Not allowing too much downtime, James gathered himself and headed for the door. There had to be a good breakfast joint close by. After some eggs, his plan was to do some work on the old homestead and then visit The Lamp and give Yvonne the news. That should be fun! *Hi, I'm out of prison, Robin is dead; what's new with you?* he thought. *Might want to work on that delivery*, he said to himself.

The combination of the cold, cloudy morning and the intermittent sleep he'd enjoyed positioned his breakfast burrito as quite possibly the best food he'd ever eaten, at least since the previous night. The food alone could keep him walking a straight path, if for no other reason than to never experience prison fare again. Hardly a noted recidivism reduction tactic, but it could be worth a look, he thought. He was thinking again. That was a good sign. James was on his third cup of black coffee and he thought with any luck he should have a pulse pretty soon. The harder he tried not to think about the night before, the more those images flooded his weary mind. He tried to pray but there was nothing. He tried to reason through the whole mess and that, too, was bankrupt. This is the dark night of the soul.

He seemed to recall an Alcoholic Anonymous meeting where he was told never to get too tired or too lonely or too something or other. No, it was don't get too hungry, angry, lonely, or tired. James laughed; he was all of these. The anger needed the most inquiry as he was unable to focus the rage on any one thing or person. He was angry with the driver of that truck, but he was also devastated to see that life wasted at a young age. He was angry with the government and the theft of his money, angry with his wife for leaving him, albeit through death. *What a selfish jerk*, he thought to himself. The reality was that he was angry with God and had no idea what to do with that dilemma. He was a pastor, he was supposed to revere and love God, not be mad at Him. Maybe the problem was trust. James felt that nobody really trusted God anyway, so why should he be any different? Oh sure, we love God and we fear God but do we trust God? No. Hold it, let's qualify that answer; we trust God for our salvation, we just don't trust Him for the rent.

The warm restaurant delayed his exit for at least thirty minutes. He was in no hurry to paint the shop; paint didn't dry well in the damp air anyway. There were a few things to buy, most notably an air bed. The sleeping bag and drop cloth had failed him miserably. A weird thought kept haunting James. He could help himself to blankets and pillows and all kinds of great stuff at Marc and Robin's house; they would want him to have whatever he needed. He first entertained that morbid notion shortly after their deaths and quite possibly the only reason he didn't take anything over then was the fear that the dogs were roaming the house. They knew him, but really? How well? He shook it from his head again, something about that whole line of thinking was just wrong and he knew it. It was like robbing graves or something equally as distasteful. Nothing a hundred bucks at Walmart couldn't remedy.

After he dropped that stuff at the shop he'd take a ride over to The Lamp and see if he could find Yvonne. She was a good friend of Robin's and deserved to hear from James and not the evening news, though he doubted that she watched much of the news. He thought about calling but that was almost as bad as watching the news. No, he'd go in person, but he made up his mind that he would not enter that building. He was in no shape to be around scantily-clad women and unlimited booze; he might never leave.

## Chapter Seventeen

It was near 3 p.m. when he carefully rode through the broken asphalt driveway that led to the newly paved parking lot of The Lamp named for Aladdin's lamp, which was the purple and yellow logo of this den of iniquity. The place was owned by a friend of the DMC and James had seen plenty of action in the joint over the years, but he knew that Saturday at 3 p.m. was a bit early for any of those guys. James parked the big Harley and placed his helmet on the seat, but kept his gloves on his hands. These places brewed trouble and there was no sense in being completely unprepared. Gloves were essential; a good belt was another helpful item. He once beat the daylights out of three guys with nothing but a belt and his notoriously quick hands. *I'm retired*, he thought.

He approached the bouncer seated on a chrome barstool with a torn red vinyl seat in front of the black metal front door. His long blonde hair appeared recently brushed and it fell purposefully on his folded arms just above the tribal design on his bicep. James resisted the urge to laugh out loud. His first thought was that this guy was posing for the cover of 'Bouncer's Monthly.' James was giving up two inches and twenty pounds but that never bothered him much. His dad would have said, 'All hat and no cattle,' James thought with a smile. "Hey, bro, I'm looking for Yvonne. Is she working today?" he asked.

"Do I know you?" the guy asked.

"Doubtful," said James.

"Then I guess we're not bro's, huh?" the bouncer added with his deepest tough guy voice.

The four or five seconds that James paused before continuing probably saved him another twenty years in the slammer. He was resisting the devil with all he had in him. As upset with himself as he was about to be for losing his cool and forgetting humility, it was better than crushing the guy's knee and then fracturing his skull with the barstool before he could uncross his arms. James had seen enough. "Yo, Fabio, go tell Yvonne that Nine Ball from the DMC is outside and wants to talk to her, NOW!" His dark eyes never wavered from the bouncer's gaze.

"Oh, crap; I'm sorry dude. I'll be back, or do you just want to go in ... I'll go get her. I'm sorry for ..."

"Get Yvonne," James said.

"Got it. I"ll get her," he said as he pulled the door open and vanished inside.

James reached down and picked up the barstool, which had suffered from the stumbling exit. Thirty seconds passed before the tough guy returned, a bit out of breath, but with news that Yvonne was on her way. "It's warm inside, bro, if you want to wait for her there," he added.

"Do I know you?" James asked.

"I'm Rick," the guy said. "I'm sorry about that back there; I was out of line," he added.

"James." He shook the tentatively outstretched hand. "I guess we're bro's now," James laughed.

"Yeah, for sure," Rick said, relieved that he wasn't going to die, at least not now.

"James, you gorgeous hunk of man!" Yvonne screamed as she jumped into James' arms and wrapped her legs around his waist. "It's so good to see you baby; you look good," she continued. "Robin said you were all buff and looking good; how you doin?"

"It's good to see you, too, Vonnie; you look as great as ever," he answered. He wasn't lying, she was late thirties and could easily pass for late twenties. He really liked the girl, but she was a complete head case. The kind of girl you'd shoot about three weeks after the wedding. Great friend but lousy long term. She was too beautiful and too wild. A man would have to fight five guys a day for the rest of his life just to be with her. He figured she had made a deal with the devil a long time ago and James kept his distance. It was tough sometimes, but thank God he never fell for this siren's song.

James took his leather and draped it over her shoulders. "Walk with me a second, Vonnie," he said softly.

"Okay, baby; where we going?" she said sweetly.

He held her hand and as he spoke, they took a few short steps, before she collapsed in his arms sobbing.

He could feel her warm tears on his cheek mixing with his as they held on to each other like they were the last two people on earth. Her hair smelled incredibly good and his mind raced as she held him. The oppression was intense; there was most certainly a devil and all men have at least one weakness. James had several, and they were all within fifty feet of him right then.

"Come inside with me," she said. "Let's get in out of the cold and have a drink and talk."

"Aww, Vonnie, I really can't. I'm doing some things differently now. I'm serving God. I know it sounds strange coming from me, but things have changed," he said.

"Robin told me you'd found religion and ... Oh, James, she's dead. Oh my God, they're gone," she said through the tears; "I can't believe this," she added, back in his arms.

"Not religion, Vonnie, Jesus. I found Jesus," he said, not meaning to sound defensive but it probably did.

"It's cool, sweetie, I think it's great. Nothing's changed for me. You're still the only guy I trust, the only guy I count on; you've always been different, a cut above all the rest. It's good you're doing this. I just don't want to lose you," she said.

James thought that was a strange thing to say after he'd just spent three years in prison without so much as a note from her and now she doesn't want to lose him? His earlier take on her was still holding water; that he'd eventually have to shoot her if he married her. He couldn't wait to get away from the place. He didn't want to spend the day in mourning; he had a different viewpoint after the last dinner conversation with Marc and Robin and the events just leading up to the crash. His friends had made their peace with God through Jesus Christ before the accident; the timing was too perfect. As much as he wanted to be grieving, there was that peace again. He was sure that none of this had caught God by surprise. Quite to the contrary, it was too lined up. It was all in His perfect plan. Michelle had told him years ago that God was more interested in their walk with him than with preserving the marriage, or the job, or the house, the car, even kids, though they never had any of their own.

God is a jealous God and it's because He's holy and He understands and loves us, even though we are clueless. It is a personal relationship with God, not a corporate worship or faith trip that the Lord is seeking with us and for us. Jesus Christ is alive and He desires to hang out with us. Go figure. "God is universal" and personal at the same time. As James stated earlier, all other religions are man's attempt to reach God, where Christianity is God's attempt to reach man.

This hit a resounding chord in James and it was this truth that was allowing him to stay at arm's length from the worldly temptations, which previously ruled his every move. This explained the peace in his spirit. If Jesus Christ, through His Holy Spirit, lived in James as in all believers, then there is an ongoing relationship as the Holy Spirit bears witness to man's spirit. James had determined that this explained this "peace which passes all understanding," and quite surely was keeping him from going crazy that very day! James jotted down his number and his address and handed it to Vonnie.

"Call me if you need anything," he said. "I better get going. I'm so sorry to bring this to you but if you were going to find out, I wanted to be the one to tell you," he said.

"I love you, James," she said as she let her head fall to his shoulder.

James simply ran his hand up her neck and grabbed her long blonde hair and kissed her on the top of her head. "Love you, too, Vonnie. Remember to call me if you need anything." He walked to his bike and turned and nodded to Rick and said, "take care of her," and slid his sunglasses on and hit the ignition. He sat on the bike and watched Yvonne as she walked into the club. She never looked back. He fastened his helmet and headed to San Bernardino. He had some painting to do.

Chapter Eighteen

Summer passed and with it, dozens of customers all benefited from James and his two part-time mechanics. He'd talked them into working odd hours that didn't interfere with their full-time positions elsewhere. After several near misses with the city, James finally obtained a business license, a business checking account, and as of the first of September, an actual paycheck, which thrilled his parole officer to no end. He even had liability insurance. As his business grew, his opportunities to minister to various persons expanded as well.

One Thursday afternoon in November as James was returning from a test ride on a recently upgraded motorcycle, he was met by two men in nice suits leaning on a 2012 Jaguar.

"You James?" the taller man asked.

"Depends," James answered, his patented response to strangers. "If you owe James money, then yes; if James owes you money, my name is Earl," to which both men laughed and assured him that he owed them nothing. "Can I get you something to drink? I have water and ... water," James said with his disarming smile.

"No thanks," said the tall guy.

"I would, actually," said the other man, a six foot tall stocky guy with a long vertical scar on his cheek.

"What can I do for you guys?" James asked.

The tall man introduced himself as Jerry Wilson and his friend, Josiah Daniels. They both owned Harleys and both desired high performance packages and they'd heard that James was the man to see. James tossed a bottle of water to Josiah and then ran through the basic options that he regularly installed: cams, adjustable push rods, fuel packs, ignition systems, handling packages, etc. The men listened to the whole pitch and settled on pretty much everything. They agreed to bring the bikes to the shop on Saturday morning.

"Can I ask you a personal question?" Jerry asked.

"You can ask," said James.

"Fair enough," Jerry said and continued. "My son, Rudy, is twenty-one-years-old and has struggled with drugs and alcohol for years. He's in prison at Chino and to be honest with you, has lost the will to live. It's really bad in there and I wondered if I could ask a huge favor; would you talk to him?"

The ticking of the big clock over James' makeshift desk could be heard loud and clear over the sudden silence. James was entertaining several thoughts: one, he was being played and they didn't need or want bike work done, and the other was how these guys knew to ask him.

"How did you know to ask me this favor, Jerry?" he asked. "I mean, why not ask the tire guy across the street or the cashier over at Costco?" his voice was rising.

"I didn't mean any disrespect; I just have nowhere to go with this," he explained.

"Who sent you to me? Who told you it was okay to talk to me about this?" James stood upright. Rage was building and he was fearful because he hadn't felt this in months and he didn't know from where it was coming. He didn't like it. His outlaw heritage made for a wary disposition. His club's motto was 'trust no one' and this visit caught him completely by surprise. James had been walking with the Lord for over two years and he was generally at peace, but once in a while a wrench would get thrown in the smooth moving gears to catch him off guard. If this was a test, James was failing miserably.

"Yvonne told me to ask you. I'm really sorry, man. I have nowhere to turn, nobody to talk to about this; it's my son!" Jerry said as tears filled his eyes. "He's my son, and I'm losing him and it's killing me," he continued.

James was moved by Jerry's candid and emotional plea, but he had to make sure he was on the level. "Would you guys excuse me for a minute?" James pulled out his phone and hit Yvonne's name and walked to the next room. "Vonnie, James; how you doin'?" he asked. "Hey, there's two guys in my shop over here driving a Jaguar and they say you sent them … You did? And you didn't call me first? What's the matter with you; did you fall on your pretty little head? Next time call me first, I don't like surprises," he said.

Yvonne calmly took her scolding and when James paused, she asked him a question, "Hey, James, honey? How's that Jesus thing working out for you?" then pushed the "end call" button on her phone.

James made a face and shook his head and yelled from the doorway, "Hey, Jerry, I lied to you earlier. I have water and coffee. You want some coffee?" he asked.

"I'd like some," Jerry answered.

"Good, I have a little story to tell you," he said as he put his arm around the stunned visitor's shoulders and led him to the customers' lounge area. "You, too, Josiah," he said. "This might take awhile."

James apologized for his behavior and told him the cliff notes version of his life and more or less how he ended up in prison and how wonderful that wasn't and what Jerry's boy was going through was normal but nonetheless hellish. He told Jerry to continue writing and visiting no matter what the kid told him and no matter how hard it was for Jerry to see his son in that place. Support is very important. James told them that he had little support as his family was mostly dead or dying when he was inside, visits from club members brought news and a few laughs, but he was quickly back to the loneliness and despair of which prison walls are constructed. He also told them that God had visited him in that cell and in retrospect he saw the need for the isolation in order for that arrangement to work itself out. James figured that had he enjoyed more visits and more distractions, he might not have been as receptive to the Lord's calling. The Bible calls it the 'still, small voice,' and it's easy to miss with the noise of the world blaring in your ears.

James agreed to write the kid a letter as he wasn't sure he could visit while on parole himself, even though he was a licensed and ordained pastor, but he would sure check it out and get back to Jerry as soon as possible. The men exchanged phone numbers and contact information for Rudy. They promised to return on Saturday with the bikes and James assured them he'd have them ready the following Friday in time for some good weekend riding.

After escorting his visitors to their car, James walked out his back door and pulled up the tattered lawn chair he kept against the building. He retrieved his pocket Bible and began to read in the book of Romans, Chapter Seven, as the apostle Paul wrote how he continued to do and say the wrong things, in spite of his desire to do right, to which James could relate:

*For what I do is not the good I want to do; no, the evil I do not want to do--this I keep on doing. Now if I do what I do not want to do, it is no longer I who do it, but it is sin living in me that does it. What a wretched man I am! Who will rescue me from this body of death? Thanks be to God through Jesus Christ our Lord! So then, I myself in my mind am a slave to God's law, but in the sinful nature a slave to the law of sin.*

He received this truth again and again and it comforted him as his flesh was often out of control and seemed to rule against his spirit, which desired to do the right thing. It was especially soothing to learn that the guy who wrote two thirds of the New Testament struggled with the same craziness that he experienced on a daily basis. With James, the problem wasn't that he didn't know what the right thing was; it was the flesh reacting so quickly sometimes that he put his foot in his mouth like he did earlier with Jerry and Yvonne, to whom he still owed an apology. It was interesting how the unsaved and worldly Yvonne was used by God to point out his shortcomings. It was interesting, too, that Paul realized exactly who would deliver him from 'this body of death;' no other than the Lord Jesus Christ who had defeated sin at the cross.

Paul said that, 'sin dwells in me,' which is fascinating, because Paul wrote this after the Lord defeated the power of sin at the cross. There is still sin. We all still sin, but Jesus Christ has conquered 'the wages of sin is death,' which frees us from the bondage of sin. Sin has been dealt with at the cross! Now we need to access the 'life' that Christ offers. His resurrection provides this life.

The average person on the street's definition or understanding of the gospel is that 'Jesus died for my sins,' or something half-baked like that. That's only half of the gospel message. If Jesus died, end of story; we'd have a tragic ending. But according to scripture, which was foretold by Old Testament prophecies, He was raised from the dead on the third day! That is good news! We appropriate the eternal life of Christ when we accept His beautiful and incredible gift of salvation. Conversely, we allow the enemy to rob us of the greatest gift of all time by focusing continually on sin instead of life. Oh yeah! *This is good stuff*, James thought.

The Lord was revealing some heavy truth to him that evening. Of course! Religion wants us to focus on sin and what we can do to earn favor with God; Christ would have us focus on Him! Focus on the abundant life he promised instead of trying to keep track of every sin. He's already handled the sin issue once and for all. This was indeed liberating. The veil of darkness was lifting from James as he read and understood for the first time the freedom that was in Christ. Knowing about God was nothing compared to knowing the person of God. James was tripping! Reading Galatians, he saw his own walk with Christ. Basically, we start out in grace and then because that's just too awesome to be true, we complicate it with legalism and rules and religion and that clogs up everything that is pure and beautiful. *Man*, he thought, Jesus must be going crazy watching us screw this all up.

He picked up the phone and called Yvonne.

"You gonna yell at me some more?" she asked, not even bothering with hello.

"No, baby, I'm gonna apologize for being an idiot," he answered.

"Took you long enough," she replied.

"It's no excuse. I'm just having a long pity party and I just decided with some help from the Lord that this party's over; just wanted to clear the air with you, babe," he explained.

"Well, I'll think about forgiving you. Come see me pretty soon, okay?" she said.

"You could come see me, too, you know," he teased.

"You never know. Thanks for calling me back. I was pretty pissed at you for a minute," she said.

"I'm sure you were. I just wanted you to know that Jesus is alive and well; it's me with the issues," he said.

"No, really?" she teased.

"Bye, Vonnie," he said.

"Love you, James," she answered.

James felt a hundred percent better after that call; she deserved better than his last attack. He was discouraged a lot of the time with his attitude and his bouts with depression. It was like he was in and out of spiritual peace and he desperately wanted to remain in a peaceful place, but life kept butting in. The trick is to trust the Lord and to remain in contact with Him. The thing James and the rest of us keep doing is pray and read and pray and read and somewhere along the way the devil comes along and suggests that we are doing pretty well and we can surely take a day or two from all that praying. God's cool, and then we take off down the hill lifting our spiritual hands from the handle bars and ... Crash! Sometimes it's a little crash and sometimes it's a big one. Most times it's a series of little crashes that parlay into one big pile of depression. We continue to focus on ourselves, which in turn makes it worse, so we focus more on ourselves and our problems and pretty soon we are mired in the quicksand of the self absorbed. It's so bad that even when we realize the problem we are powerless to pull ourselves out! It's all about us! And we've been the problem all along.

We need to focus on the Lord and the ministry He has for us, which is always about ministering to others. But, how does ministering to others get us out of our mess? The enemy will continue to remind us that our problems are still there and we'd better quit fooling around with ministry and helping others and get back to work on our problems. No! Here's the trick; God will fix our problems only if we will get the heck out of the way. We should not become amateur providences and continue to interfere with God, like He needs our help or something. That's insane.

Chapter Nineteen

James figured he'd been outside reading for a bit over two hours — pure immersion in the word of God — and the time passed quickly but fully. He hadn't read for that length of time since Folsom and that was primarily to escape his brutal reality. He read Romans and Galatians and pieces of James (of course) as well as Jude and part of Acts. He was a big Apostle Paul fan and figured he'd have gotten along with that guy pretty well. He looked forward to meeting him someday. James figured that Paul would get kicked out of just about any church he attended in Southern California and probably any church in America. He had Paul pegged as a biker for sure. That thought stayed with him awhile.

Maybe James should start a church. Ella had certainly suggested it on more than one occasion, the first being that fateful night at the Olive Garden and the most recent just a couple of days ago at the Sunday evening Bible study on the one-year anniversary of the 'little' study, which had grown from the original five participants to fifty-six people. James was forever grateful that he kept the engagement even though it was also the anniversary of the wreck that had stolen his friends from him. He never questioned God over the timing, but he often thought how much Marc and Robin would have loved the food and fellowship at Bria's house. It was so contagious that even Bud had started attending in the spring and hadn't missed a Sunday since. Good for him, James thought.

Bud had become a great friend and an even better landlord. Together they had rehabbed the building into a nice-looking contemporary storefront, so much so that several other owners had begun similar restorations, giving that side of the street some new life. It was a reflection of the power emanating from the bike shop. Things were good, God was good, His blessings were everywhere, yet James continued his private battle with depression. He knew the source, but it didn't make it any easier to combat. He called it "depression from oppression."

~

Permission to visit Jerry's son was easier than he anticipated. He was, after all, a licensed and ordained

251

pastor. Matter of fact, he could just walk in with a simple appointment. His parole officer was actually complimentary, and mumbled something about James turning into a good Christian man. James thanked him as he reviewed the final paperwork for his pending release. It was a relief to be removing that stigma from his legal status. Being a business owner on parole was easier than having to explain it to every potential employer, nonetheless parole was something he was happy to have behind him. He officially had another five weeks, and one more appointment that would basically be an official discharge and would take all of five minutes, but the state wanted to inconvenience him once more by mandating his appearance.

James had mixed emotions. He was certainly glad to be done with all of this, but the end of parole meant that the DMC would be expecting and planning his return to royalty. He was an officer in the club with mad cred. He could write his own ticket and live large as the legendary Nine Ball. There would no doubt be a weekend long party in his honor with mandatory attendance by all members from all chapters. The club had grown to over four hundred members in seven states in the four years since he'd been active in the club. They were a force to be reckoned with for sure. James had witnessed packs of over fifty bikes thundering down Interstate 10, and another time while heading south on Interstate 15 from the high desert spotted well over a hundred DMC rolling north, most likely to Vegas to descend on that well-deserving town. Ignoring them was not an option and truth be told, James wasn't sure how he was going to deal with the pending showdown. He was told a long time ago that you could be an outlaw Christian, but not a Christian outlaw.

The meaning wasn't exactly clear then, but he figured it meant that you could be an outsider, a different kind of Christian but never a ruthless, law-breaking marauder masquerading as a Christian. If it ever came down to Christ or the Club, there would be no hesitation; he was sold out for Jesus. There would never be a compromise. James was struggling with trying to live two lives. Was it possible to be an uncompromising Christian and belong to an outlaw motorcycle club? He didn't see how. He had relegated these thoughts to the back of his mind for almost a year, but it was clear that he had better begin thinking and praying his way out of this difficult confrontation. Or should it be praying, then thinking?

He knew all too well that nobody just walked away from the DMC. A man could surely be kicked out, but walk out? Not likely. Not if he wanted to sleep peacefully ever again. An MC is a marriage; sometimes it's a bad marriage, but you don't talk bad about your spouse and you sure as heck don't ask for a divorce. There was no doubt in his mind that it would come down to the club or his faith and as strong as his faith was at times, he was just a man and with that came weakness and fear. He'd enjoyed the peace he'd been allowed the past year. Loneliness had crept in on occasion, especially the weeks and months just after the accident, but for the most part he used that time for prayer and study. He'd grown to understand and accept that the Lord was real and His spirit lived in him as with all born-again believers and that spirit offered peace and power, albeit a different brand of power than he'd known in the world. Spiritual strength was more subtle but possessed far higher octane than its counterfeit worldly counterpart. It just took time to appropriate that power and now that James was experiencing it he had a fighting chance to defeat all that was coming at him. The key was knowing how and when to back away in the flesh and allow God to be God.

People, men especially, have been taught their whole lives to be strong and not rely on anyone else. Then Jesus comes along and says just the opposite. It takes faith, and lots of it, to fully rely on God. It would take all James could muster in the few short weeks before all hell would break loose in San Bernardino County. He was trying to imagine a life with no power, no status, and perhaps even no money as the DMC could put a guy out of business with one word. James would be put to the test, that was for sure. He sighed knowing that he did have a few weeks to pray up and get ready for the showdown. He laughed to himself because anyone else on the planet would be thrilled to be off parole, yet he was dreading the consequences. It figured!

In the meantime, he was plenty busy for November. The shop had several jobs winding down that week, the two from Jerry and Josiah would arrive on Saturday, plus three others were slated to start mid next week. The Lord had certainly blessed him with work and it seemed every customer would send him another. Of course, there was the star factor or what James referred to as the petting zoo' effect, where people would bring their bikes to him because he was Nine Ball from the DMC and if he worked on your bike and you talked to him then you were friends, and of course, you could now drop his name at some run or over coffee at the next free hotdog day at your local motorcycle dealer. James understood that curiosity and just shrugged and took the business and used every opportunity to tell people that it was God who pulled him from the mire and put his feet on the rock. Some of those customers showed up on Sunday nights and ended up bringing friends. James enjoyed those referrals best of all.

Chapter Twenty

A couple of days before Christmas, Bud asked James to take a drive with him to look at a new property he was considering. James had both of his mechanics in the shop that morning so he figured it would be nice to get out with Bud and get some coffee and take an hour for his friend. Bud was particularly goofy and James chalked it up to the Christmas spirit. James could only smile along with the guy, such was his level of enthusiasm. *The Bible studies and expanded social contact were doing wonders for the man,* James thought. Bud was rambling on and on about how everyone except James knew that God had a bigger ministry for him and if he'd just quit being a moody jerk maybe God could utilize him more extensively. James continued in his silence, inwardly thrilled that Bud was so 'on fire' for the Lord, as this was exactly what James had in mind when he agreed to head up the Bible studies on Sunday nights.

Bud pulled into a parking lot facing a large warehouse with a nice facade in front which gave it the appearance of a high end office building. "What do you think?" he asked.

"Looks nice. Pretty big for your tastes, isn't it?" James asked.

"I have the lockbox combination; you want to look inside?" Bud asked, ignoring James' comment.

"Sure, why not."

The place was impressive upon entry with its vaulted ceiling and stairway leading to the upstairs offices. It was obviously a new building. The smells of fresh paint and new carpet greeted the men as they continued the tour upstairs. The upper level boasted eight large offices and a huge conference room, which led to a large kitchen and break room.

"What the heck would you do with a place like this?" James asked, obviously impressed by the tour.

"Split it up, maybe three or four businesses. Wait till you see the warehouse area," Bud replied.

The men headed down the stairs, which faced another stairway across the large tiled foyer under a beautiful chandelier.

Once inside the warehouse, James was awed by its size. "This must be twenty-five thousand square feet down here," he commented.

"Thirty thousand, but who's counting," laughed Bud. "I can divide this warehouse up as well. I think it's a great place for your new church, don't you?" he asked as he walked ahead of James.

"Maybe someday, Bud," James said without a clue where his friend was leading him.

"Why wait? You could take half of this place and put on quite a Saturday night service like the one you keep telling me about," Bud said.

"Dude, I couldn't afford a place like this. Like I said, someday maybe," James answered.

"You had fifty-six people at the last Bible study and if you could get ten dollars a week from each of them you'd have this rent easy," Bud continued.

"Yeah, but that's a big if," James said.

"Where's your faith, James?" Bud asked, reaching his hand over to his younger friend's shoulder. "You have been called by God to preach, my friend. I know it and everyone who knows you knows it, so take the leap. I've got your back. I got a terrific price on this place, I can rent most of it to you and the rest to some other Monday through Friday businesses and you'll have everything in one place. You can move the other shop over here, too. I can rent it out easily now that you've fixed it all up," Bud said with a laugh. "Whaddya say, James; let's do this. I know it's the right thing," Bud was on a roll. "I will get the keys in a week. You won't have to pay first and last or a security deposit. It's my Christmas present to you, you can't say no."

"You're sure about this?" James asked with tears now beyond the I've-got-something-in-my-eye stage.

"I've never been more sure of anything. God used you to bring me into the kingdom and now I've got the ability to help you and I'm going to whether you want it or not," Bud said.

James pulled his friend to him and hugged him. He held on for a minute, then gathered himself and looked right at Bud with bright red eyes and said, "Merry Christmas."

Bud let out a yell, which echoed through the empty stadium of a warehouse. After a quick look around the outside of the building, the men hopped back into the pickup truck and rolled back to the shop.

Bud waved the bright red mini cooper into the driveway and slowly rolled to his customary parking spot in the gravel to the left of the shop. The tall redhead who emerged from the tiny car waved at the two of them and reached to grab something from the passenger's seat. James and Bud looked at each other as if to say, *Who is that?* Once she came closer, James recognized her as Linda, the bank manager.

"What brings you to the other side of the tracks?" James asked.

"Oh please, this place looks awesome! I shop at Costco almost weekly and I've noticed all the work you guys have done over here. It really looks great," she said, shaking James' hand. "Happy Holidays," she said and handed James a package of nuts and assorted snacks.

"Merry Christmas," James responded.

"Merry Christmas to you. I'm so used to the politically correct greeting we're encouraged to use at the bank," she said.

"Yeah, well we're the least politically correct stop you'll make today," James answered.

"We keep Christ in Christmas around here," Bud said as James laughed and introduced the two.

"That's refreshing," she said.

"Let me show you around, though it looks like I'll be moving my operation up the road a mile or so very soon," he said, winking at Bud.

"Nice to meet you, Linda," Bud said. "I have to get over to Lowe's; if I don't spend some money over there pretty soon they are going to start worrying about me."

"You, too, Bud, Merry Christmas," Linda said.

Bud made a weird up-and-down movement with his eyebrows that only James could see and James had to turn away to keep from laughing.

"I'll see you later, Bud. Thanks for the nice present, bro," James said.

"Okay, my pleasure," he said, and off he walked to that darn Ford truck, which seemed to get stronger every day.

"I should never have sold that truck," James said. "Come on in; you want some coffee?" he gestured to the front door with a sweeping move of his arm.

"I'd love some," she said.

After a quick tour — it was only three rooms after all — they sat in the shop and drank coffee and talked for almost an hour. James gave Linda the best padded shop stool in the place while he leaned against his work bench and found conversation effortless with this beautiful and funny lady. She even liked motorcycles. James told her his whole story and emphasized the past year and especially the great news about the new building and the study group and how excited he was to enlist their help in building a new fellowship in a great new building. James was more excited and joyous than he'd been in … well, longer than he could remember.

Linda was perfect. She was engaging and witty and brilliant. She shared his enthusiasm for the new church and agreed that Bud's invitation was too good to pass up. James invited her to attend and she happily accepted. She actually seemed disappointed to have to return to the bank and James, without much thought, asked her to join him for dinner soon. Linda quickly agreed. Then James broke out in laughter and Linda asked what was so darn funny and he said, "Do we take the Cooper or the bike?" which Linda thought was hilarious. James found himself quite taken by this woman and thanked her for coming by and promised he would call very soon. He walked her to the car and shook her hand, taking a long look into her green eyes and thinking that the day was a pretty good day so far. As a cam and pushrod job was waiting for him inside, he shook off the green-eyed lady and went back to the comfort of the little shop. A quick adjustment on the XM radio and the volume provided the proper environment for the completion of the project. He lost himself in the right side of the Harley for a couple of blissful hours.

With a strange feeling that he was being watched, James looked up from the engine to see Yvonne's beautiful form appear in his doorway. Her wavy blonde hair contrasted her chocolate brown dress. "Vonnie, this is a nice surprise. What's up?" He stood up and walked toward her embrace.

"Hi, sweetie. So this is the shop. I love it," she said as her eyes surveyed the surroundings.

"Let me show you around," he said. *This must be ladies day*, he thought.

The three-minute tour covered his humble shop and his sleeping area and the microwave and the refrigerator from which he pulled two bottles of water. The last room on the tour was the stately bathroom to which Yvonne simply turned to James and said, "Where did this come from?"

James laughed and told her it was like that when he got the place and he was as surprised as she was when he opened the little door. "What you gonna do?" he asked with smile.

"Keep it; it's awesome," she answered.

"So, were you just in the neighborhood or what?" James asked.

"I just missed you," she said.

James just looked at her with his patented look and said, "What's really going on?"

She held out her hand, "They asked me to come by and give you this," she said and handed James a flyer for a huge DMC party scheduled for January seventh. It was called 'Nine Ball Tournament' and it was going to be a blowout with all chapters and supporters encouraged to attend. James knew that encouraged to attend was DMC for 'mandatory' and you had better darn well be there. It was to be held at the Badlands in Yucaipa, of course.

"Nine Ball Tournament; very creative," he said.

"I thought so, too," she said. "It's quite an honor, James; they are pulling out all the stops for your return," she added, her eyes searching his for a clue as to his temperature on this party.

James had already figured the DMC sent her personally to get a read on his reaction as it wouldn't have been too difficult for a 'hang around' to drop this off or tape it to his front door. No, these guys were always manipulating, scheming, doing everything short of just asking a brother what's up. They definitely got the jump on him with this approach. There would be no quiet sit-down the day he completed parole; this public display was their way of saying 'you're back and you're not going anywhere,' and there was nothing James could do about it, at least without causing a massive incident that would only make it more difficult to pull away. He would have to attend and play nice.

Conscious of her gaze, James simply said, "You're right, babe; it's quite an honor. I'll have to buy a new black shirt."

"You look great in black, sweetie," she said.

"Guess I'll see you there," he said. "I better get back to work and finish this bike by tonight; I have a couple more coming in tomorrow. I appreciate you coming here and bringing this; it's extra nice getting to see you."

Yvonne stepped up and kissed him hard on the mouth and for the second time in ten minutes James was surprised by her. He pulled back and said, "Wow, you made my day twice now."

"You wanna make it three times?" she teased.

"Better not, Vonnie, I'm an old man. You might kill me," he said nervously.

"You're sure now? I'll be gentle," she said.

"You just be there on the seventh," he said, attempting to diffuse the moment.

"Okay, but this hard-to-get act is making you even more desirable you know, and there's no way I'm missing your party," she laughed.

"Yeah, good; my plan is working," James smiled, relieved as she headed out the front door. James hugged her and kissed her on the forehead as she slipped into her Corvette. "Thanks again, Vonnie, see you soon," he said.

Ten seconds later she accelerated out of the driveway and off to her dark cave or wherever she stayed in the daylight hours. He walked into the shop and poured himself a cup of hours-old coffee and hit it hard. It was tepid and terrible but it would be a good four hours before he finished up the cams and pushrods on this bike. He quickly nuked the remaining coffee to an acceptable temperature. It would take awhile to shake her memory from his brain. This woman was an eleven on a one-to-ten scale and his flesh was waging thermonuclear war with his spirit right now. He took a long pull from the heated coffee.

"Arrrggghh!" he yelled. "Okay, I'm all better now," he laughed and headed to the motorcycle, which was suspended on the lift about three feet from the ground. "Back to work," he said. Marshall Tucker's "Can't you see" was playing on the stereo and James laughed and looked to the high ceiling and said, "You got that right, Lord!"

# Chapter Twenty-One

Kit could install an exhaust system drunk and blindfolded, but for some reason he'd ridden out from Orange County with his new exhaust strapped to his sissy bar. James was surprised to see him roll up with Tio unannounced, aside from a recent phone call that ended with Kit saying, "maybe we'll come out to see your shop sometime."

James had called Kit a couple of weeks after the accident. He wasn't sure why, but after a few days of the Lord's prompting, James figured he'd better call if for no other reason than to see what the Lord wanted with him and those Prophets that he'd met at the gas station. James sure liked those guys, but he hardly knew them well enough to call. He was wrong about that; Kit and the rest of the club assured him that he was more than welcome at their clubhouse any time and had encouraged James to attend the mid-week Bible study, which he did on a couple of occasions. They had developed a friendship, though James had heretofore not mentioned his affiliation with the DMC.

James met the two in the doorway and exchanged hugs and pleasantries before Kit mentioned that he'd just purchased the exhaust and asked if James could fit him in to install it. James ordinarily scheduled everything and rarely stuck random jobs into the mix, but since it was Kit he said, "Sure, bro; roll it around and we can take care of it right away."

James was looking for an opportunity to breach the subject of his DMC affiliation and that morning was as good a time as any. He felt strange about telling these guys, especially since he'd known them for months now and, what, it just slipped his mind that he was an officer in one of the most notorious outlaw clubs on the west coast and oops, *I forgot to tell you guys, I hope that doesn't change anything.* "You'll need to map these pipes to get the most out of them. One of my guys will be here in an hour for this other job, but we could get him to do yours if you have the time today," James told Kit.

"Yeah, bro, I have the time. I appreciate you doing this on short notice. I got these pipes from a guy over in Redlands and Tio had your address so we just thought we'd stop. Hope we're not keeping you from anything more important." Kit said.

"Not a problem; it's good to see you guys again. I always enjoy you guys, lots of laughs; you Prophets are funny cats," James said.

"We do have fun," Tio said.

"I'm on parole for another few days. I think I told you guys a few months ago that I just got out in January," James said.

"Yeah, good deal on the parole, bro; it'll be great to be clear," Kit said.

"Oh, yeah, for sure. What I didn't mention and I don't know why, but I'm with the Doomsayers MC, but conditions wouldn't allow any affiliation for a year, so I'm always ridin' solo," James explained.

"Yeah, you're Nine Ball; huh, bro?" Tio asked.

James looked up at the two smiling brothers and they all started laughing. "You guys knew all along?"

"Well, yeah, one of our brothers thought he'd seen you before when we all met up that day at the gas station. We figured you'd tell us when you felt like it; makes no difference to us either way, bro. You're a brother in the Lord and we're honored to fellowship with you any way any time. We're cool with the DMC. We do funerals and weddings and hospital visits for everyone; we've been at Loma Linda a few times for some of your downed brothers. We've got no beef with anyone and nobody's got a beef with us," Kit said.

"Except the other Christian clubs," Tio said with a serious face, then he and Kit laughed long and hard. "Not really, bro; we love everyone!" Tio said.

James just loved being around these guys and this was the kind of thing that kept him coming back. They were humble and they thought nothing of themselves. They were honored to serve the Lord and made themselves available to any and all clubs for ministry opportunities. They were certainly busier than the outlaw clubs as there were always brothers in need.

A couple of hours later Kit was roaring up and down the street smiling like a kid at Christmas. Not only did the bike sound great but it had more jump and Kit was always looking for more speed. It was a standing joke in their club nobody could outrun the "P." James insisted on the work as a Christmas present as long as the Prophets would bless him with attending the new church and showing up at the party at the Badlands. They agreed.

As the new year was a couple of days away, James figured he had some unfinished business in Chino and since the weather was cooperating he might as well take a ride. He almost selected Joe Bonamassa's first album for accompaniment but settled at the last minute on an AM radio preacher who was teaching from Romans, Chapter Five: 'For while we were still weak, at the right time, Christ died for the ungodly. For one will scarcely die for a righteous person—though perhaps for a good person one would dare to even die—but God shows his love for us in that, while we were still sinners, Christ died for us.'

The volume must have been pretty loud as people glanced at him at stoplights, trying not to stare but nonetheless aware of the preaching. Since bikers sometimes refer to their bikes as their mount, like a horse, James' twisted sense of humor thought this could be the 'sermon on the mount.' James thought to turn down the volume but then laughed to himself and said, *They need it, too.* James thought it incomprehensible how much God loved us then and loves us now. He tried to imagine how God could send his only son to die for those who would spit on him and curse him.

~

James negotiated the gauntlet of red tape that served to detour impromptu visitations but with his clergy status, things settled pretty quickly. He was instructed to proceed to and wait at station six where the prisoner would meet him after being summoned.

The months had been unkind to the prisoner. The kid's face was thinner, his eyes a bit more hollow than when they locked with James' eyes through the frame of the backseat window back in January. James collapsed onto the hard stool that faced the glass partition separating him from his friend's killer. *This is awkward*, he thought. He slowly shook his head as he recalled the sermon on the way here. *You are amazing, Lord*, he thought. Words escaped him; he tried desperately to maintain his composure and reach deep for the scriptures about loving your enemy. He just stared at the kid and felt the anguish of that night all over again. A half a minute or so passed before he reached for the scratched-up black phone to his right. He thought about a guy he worked with years ago who sprayed Lysol on every phone he used. The kid mirrored his movement and they just stared at each other with phones to their ears. It was progress.

"So how's your sobriety coming along?" James asked wryly.

"Great. There's no night life in here to speak of," the kid answered.

"Word," James answered. "You remember me?"

"Should I?" the kid answered.

James quickly deduced the thickness of the glass and the futility of trying to get to this disrespectful little punk, so he continued, "I was there that night. I looked right at you in the back of that cop's car. Those were my friends you killed."

Rudy lost the stare down as he slowly hung his head. "Why are you here?" he asked.

"That's a good question. I sure didn't expect to see you, that's for sure. Your dad asked me to talk to you, and he obviously didn't know either," James said. "It's pretty safe to say I wouldn't have come if I had known it was you, but since we're past that little hurdle ... here I am."

"Yeah, my dad told me you might come by. I don't know why he's asking perfect strangers to visit me."

"I ain't perfect, but they don't get much stranger," James replied.

"So, you gonna tell me that everything's gonna be okay and all that?" Rudy asked.

"Hardly," James replied.

They sat there for another uncomfortable length of time before Rudy said, "You can leave, dude; I won't blame you."

"You won't blame me? That's good of you 'cause I sure as heck blame you! I hope you freaking rot in here, but they'll no doubt let you out in a couple of years so you can go waste someone else's life."

"I doubt it; I got twelve years. I'll be transferred up north somewhere soon," Rudy said.

"Twelve years for killing two people? That ain't bad at all, Rudy. You'll do half of that. You've got time served, and you'll be out in five, mark my words," James said. "That's how it works and that part ain't your fault, so the way I see it you've got five years to get your head straight and get right with the Lord. Make something of your life instead of sitting here crying to daddy that your poor messed-up little life has gotten uncomfortable. I'll bet a hundred bucks that your daddy bought you that nice truck you used to kill my friends, 'cause if you had worked for it you wouldn't have wrecked it," he barked.

"Screw you," said Rudy. He slammed down the receiver and disappeared down the stark white hallway, his orange jumpsuit fading into a sea of inmates leaving the visitors area.

"That went well," James said out loud as he stood up and headed out. He was feeling pretty righteous about that little encounter, mumbling how much more he'd like to tell that little punk, what a piece of crap he was, etc. James started his bike and a different preacher seemed to pick right up where the last one left off … how it's no big deal treating your friends with love, but try it with some punk kid who, in a moment of drunken stupidity … not unlike the several hundred times James himself could have done the same thing, committed a crime that would haunt him the rest of his life.

It ruined the ride home and the rest of his day. How the heck could he feel that bad about going off on the idiot who killed his friends? That was totally insane. Time was he wouldn't have thought twice about beating the life out of the kid and then spend the night drinking and playing pool; now he felt bad for yelling at the guy. "All right, Lord, I'll go see him again in a couple of days. I'm sure this will bug me until I do."

~

James cursed as he tripped over the bike lift getting to his cell phone vibrating near the edge of the work bench. "Yeah, James," he answered.

"It's Jerry; how you doing?" the voice said.

"Okay. What's up? How's the bike running?" James asked, although he was pretty sure the bike wasn't the reason for the call.

"It's great, seems to get better the more I ride it," Jerry answered. "The bike's fine. I'm calling about Rudy," he said.

"Yeah, well, I'm sure he told you that the visit didn't go so well," James said.

"Yeah, I know why and I called to tell you how sorry I am. I can't believe this whole thing and I never would have asked you had I known. I apologize," Jerry said.

"It's not your fault; I wasn't prepared for all possibilities. I surely could have handled it better; he's just a kid. Going off like I did didn't help," James explained.

"Yeah, well, he deserved it … God knows I could have been a stronger figure in his life."

"Don't go there, Jerry; you're a good father. You're there for him and you love him. Kids grow up and gotta make their own decisions. I'm sure it's hard on you, too," James said in his best pastoral tone.

"Rudy said he fully understands why you said what you said, he wanted me to tell you something, though, for what it's worth. He said to tell you that you were right about the truck," Jerry said. "I don't know what that means but he asked that I not forget to tell you that."

"Just an inside joke with Rudy and me," James said. "I'll get out and see him again this week; we can start over," James said.

"I can't ask you to do that," Jerry cried.

"It's out of our hands, Jerry. I'm dealing with God on this one and if I want any peace in my stinking life I have to go back there," James laughed. "Don't sweat it; it'll work out. I'll call you when I get back," James said.

"Thanks; I look forward to your call," Jerry replied.

"Go ride your bike!" James laughed. He felt a little better, but he knew he needed to get over to Chino pretty soon. The DMC party was in three days and

James wanted the Rudy visit done by then. He needed a clear head for that nightmare.

Chapter Twenty-Two

"I'm not into the God thing, dude; you're wasting your time," Rudy said with a smirk. "God is for weak people who aren't in control of their own destiny," he continued.

"I'm out here, idiot; you're the one with wasted time! You're in charge of your destiny and this is the best you could come up with?" James laughed, waving his arm, showing Rudy the prison visitors area. "I'm not sure I'd be bragging about this, brother!"

Rudy slammed down the phone and started to leave. James jumped up and smashed the meaty side of his fist against the glass and yelled, "Get your ass back here!" He must have looked like a patient at the state hospital pounding on the soundproof glass, his mouth wide open but no sound on Rudy's side.

Rudy flipped him off, but then sat back down and grabbed the phone. "You're crazy!" he yelled.

"Really, alert the media," James yelled back.

Several other visitors nervously looked over at James. He lowered his voice and said, "Look dude, gas ain't cheap. I've gotta make this visit worth it, so let's agree not to abruptly terminate the conversation anymore. We both seem to have trouble with intimacy."

"Fine. I ain't in no hurry to return to the resort just yet; they haven't finished cleaning the pool," Rudy said with his first smile.

"Fair enough," James answered. "Can I tell you something about my time at Folsom? Maybe we can arrive at a place where we can have a discussion instead of what we've been doing," James asked.

"Yeah, I guess so," Rudy said.

James talked for about ten minutes and it felt like three. Rudy was wide-eyed when James told him who he was and how he arrived in the seat opposite Rudy. Turns out the street cred gained from being an officer in the DMC worked pretty well on twenty-one-year-olds. James inwardly hoped that being a former member would work just as well. He had to trust God for that situation. He would know soon enough.

James was careful not to glamorize the outlaw world too much, as it was not his intention to send

Rudy careening in that direction. The kid was pretty terrified in his current surroundings, so seeing that reality and the knowledge that prisons and cemeteries were the final resting places of most outlaws should deter him from that career path. "Can I tell you something without you hanging up on me?" James asked.

"Maybe," Rudy answered.

"In my experience, people who aren't into the 'God thing,' as you put it, are really just not interested in being held accountable for their actions. If there's a God, then we have a high bar as far as our behavior; you follow me?" James asked.

Rudy was silent but nodded.

James continued, "If you look at things honestly, which is what I finally had to do, bro, we all get to that point where we can't explain it away anymore. The Bible says we all know there's a God; we just willingly ignore and reject Him. That's pretty heavy, if you ask me," James stopped to get a gauge on his subject. Rudy just stared at him. "So here's my answer to the most popular objections to the Bible; you ready?" he asked.

"Go for it," Rudy replied.

"To those who brush aside the Bible as God's word by saying it's just written by men, I say they're right. It was written by men, forty of them over two thousand years, sixty-six books, and they all pointed to Jesus Christ as the Messiah. If you can show me how that could happen outside of the inspiration of God, I'll break you out of here myself." Rudy laughed as James finished his thought. "Dude, saying that men wrote the Bible actually only proves how amazing God is.

"The second objection I hear is that the authors of the gospels just corroborated their stories to further their agendas. The gospels of Matthew, Mark, Luke, and John were written at different times from differing perspectives. Even liberal scholars can agree on that point. Each of them told varying but generally similar stories — some parts were in all gospels, some were only in one or two — but the big stuff, the virgin birth, the perfect sinless life and the death and resurrection are all there. Some of these guys were actually eyewitnesses. I don't need to tell you how damaging an eyewitness can be." James stopped for effect as Rudy rolled his eyes.

"You're too young to remember the Watergate story, but back in the seventies some dudes broke into the Democratic National headquarters. Looking back, it was an insanely stupid thing to do as the Republicans were gonna crush George McGovern anyway. Regardless, these idiots got caught and one by one they gave each other up under the threat of minimal prison time and bad publicity. Nothing life-threatening mind you, but every last one of the co-conspirators rolled over on the next guy to save their sorry butts. Rewind a couple thousand years to the dudes who ran with Jesus. Those guys had real reasons to flip. Almost every one of them was killed in a most horrible manner because they wouldn't change their story about what Jesus told them and what they witnessed. Torture and death wouldn't make these guys change their stories; you think maybe they all believed what they were saying?"

Rudy looked at James and indicated yes. In fact, he said, "I never thought of it like that."

James continued. "Most people don't think about any of it, bro; they are too busy watching their flat screens and drinking beer." Rudy smiled and James held his finger up to the window and said, "Don't go there," and Rudy smiled some more.

"One more thing to ponder. Jesus' brother, James, was the biggest unbeliever of all. I mean think about it; do you have a brother, Rudy?" James asked.

"No, a big sister, no brother," he answered.

"What do you think your sister would say if you told her you were God?" James asked.

"She'd call the asylum," Rudy laughed.

"Exactly, though I'm sure Jesus was a darn sight better brother than you were," James said. Rudy flipped him off through the window. James just looked at him until Rudy acquiesced with a shrug suggesting he would stipulate to Jesus being a better brother. "My point, dude, is that after Jesus was crucified and rose from the dead, he appeared to James. Next thing you know, James is Mr. Church leader and was a great early Christian warrior for the cause. When you investigate the claims of Christ and His followers, you'll arrive at a conclusion that will astound you. Don't be afraid to press this; the word of God has held up under scrutiny for centuries. You ain't gonna scare Him by asking some questions. I'm gonna split now. You think about what we talked about, bro; come up with some original thought if you can without hurting your saturated little brain and I'll be back soon."

Rudy flipped him off again and said, "You're real funny. You're really coming back, huh?"

James saw a little child through the window, worried that he was being left alone. It could have been at the bus stop as a kindergartner or at the babysitter's house when his parents were going to dinner, but every little kid has that fear and this kid still showed his. "Yeah, bro, I'll be back. Take care of yourself, stay quiet, lay low; you'll be okay," James said.

"Okay, man, see ya," Rudy said in his best tough guy voice.

Both phones hit their respective receivers simultaneously. The men stared at each other for a second before they went their very separate ways. James had a feeling that this kid would be hard to shake. God had a long assignment planned and it was a great feeling knowing that he had a task, one for which James would have never have been a willing volunteer. He was witnessing God's wonderful and mysterious methodology and he was in awe. "Thank you, Jesus," James whispered as he walked toward his motorcycle. The dark clouds and cold wind had been building while he was inside; it was time to hit the road.

## Chapter Twenty-Three

James rolled down the grade that led to the street entrance of the Badlands Bar in Yucaipa. He looked on in amazement at the sheer number of motorcycles and people lining his route. There were already hundreds of them. He quickly realized that his flyer had a later time posted than for the rest of the revelers. They wanted a welcome fit for a returning hero. James was overwhelmed. He had tried to prepare himself for any type of reception, but this was beyond anything he had imagined.

By the time he had stroked the kickstand into position, the toilet paper streamers were everywhere. People were in the trees, on top of the building, and around the parking lot, tossing dozens of rolls toward James. The cheering was intense, like a concert and it kept building until he thought it would end and then it built some more. People were pouring out of the bar, all clapping and yelling until the six foot seven inch tall Snake, the P, walked out with Tramp and Stitch, who carried Nine Ball's cut like a linen napkin over his arm.

The noise was deafening as they extended the colors to James and he slid into that cut like a tailored glove.

"Yeah!!" Snake yelled and grabbed James and hugged him like a bear, spinning him around as James' feet left the ground. Just then over four hundred Doomsayers patch holders ran out of the bar in a line, all of them yelling with arms raised. It took a full five minutes for them to assemble outside. Anyone other than Snake would have needed a microphone and a stage but his head and loud voice towered over everyone. The cheering died down as he raised both arms like a quarterback on the goal line asking for silence. "DMC NATION!! Our Brother is HOME!! LET'S GET IT ON!"

This time the noise took on a crazed sound, chanting and pounding like a conquering army thirsting for more. James only recognized a quarter of the people at this party-turned-bacchanal and as much as he was lifted up and saluted, he felt strangely detached.

Samantha was still there tending bar, but she had three assistants today as the Badlands had never seen this type of crowd before. "Hi, James," she yelled over the three-deep line at the bar.

"Step aside," yelled a deep voice. "Nine Ball in the house!" and the crowd parted to allow James access to the pretty bartender who was extending two bottles of his previous favorite brew.

He hugged her over the bar and yelled, "Iced tea with lemon, okay, honey?"

Samantha took a step back and said, "Yeah? Okay, baby, you da man; Iced tea it is. You gonna be at the tables? I'll send it right over. It's so good to see you back!" she yelled.

"Thanks, yeah, table two, as usual," he yelled back at her. Complete strangers and old buddies were pounding him on the back; it was complete mayhem and James was in shock to see the ocean of Doomsayers MC patches rolling through the building and flowing outside. The Badlands had a back patio which was, to his recollection, never used for much more than a storage area, but tonight it was decorated with tiki torches and fake palm trees as a makeshift tropical paradise. He made a note to have a cigar out there later.

James arrived at his favorite pool table where two guys were already playing a spirited game of eight ball.

Two patch holders walked up to the guys and said, "Game's over," and took the cue ball and pointed at James.

"No, no, let them finish; I'll play the winner, "James said. He nodded to the patch holders. "It's cool, thanks," as they returned the ball to the table.

They in turn looked over the rail to the sergeant-at-arms as if to say, *we tried*, and he just nodded to them. James was being watched and followed by everyone tonight there would be no relaxing games of pool this evening.

"There he is," yelled the familiar voice of his favorite vixen. Vonnie had everything planned tonight, even the ruby-colored high heels that matched her very classy just above the knee, dress.

*Oh crap*, he thought; *This is not good.*

She stopped the room as she moved toward James and hung on his neck with both feet off the ground. "You smell great," she said.

"You're stunning." He couldn't think of a better word.

"I'm all yours," she whispered. She was pushing twelve on the scale and she had him on a laser lock. It would take everything he had to avoid her and the more he saw of her, the weaker he got.

The night wore on and the crowd got louder and crazier. The noise of the brothers racing up and down the street was non-stop as each chapter put its fastest bikes out there for bragging rights. Later the boys would square off in a makeshift boxing ring and beat the daylights out of each other to determine the toughest Chapter. James won it all ten years ago, but he wouldn't be entering the fray that night; he was done fighting for the sake of fighting. He'd go if he had to, that was for sure, but he was tired of waking up in pain for no good reason. He had held the pool table for over two hours when he decided to take a break.

"You guys take over," he said to some onlookers. "I need a break."

James had no sooner left the table when Yvonne appeared out of nowhere. "Where do you think you're going, sugar?" she asked.

"Just out for some air; wanna come?"

"Absolutely," she said and grabbed his hand.

James and Vonnie had always been friends but he was noticing a weird vibe that night; she was clingy and Vonnie was never that. She never had to be; guys would kill to be with her and she knew it. It was strange but he had to admit, it was nice. In the back of his mind, however, something had him on alert with regard to Vonnie.

They headed out to the Tiki Lounge when two patch holders approached James with the news that the Prophets were at the front door at his invitation. James excused himself from Vonnie quickly, as he knew the sooner everyone saw him embrace the Prophets, the sooner they would be welcomed and safe in this crazy place. He made his way to the front where six Prophets, including Kit and Tio, were standing, showing respect by not entering the building. In that split second he had the vision.

James hugged Kit and Tio and the rest and quickly introduced them to Snake and a few others, and then invited them in. He made it clear that the Prophets were honored guests and were to be treated as such. He even introduced them to Vonnie. It would have been hard not to as she was attached to James at the hip. He knew from his earlier discussions that they wouldn't stay long and it was out of respect for James that they showed up at all. This was not their usual choice of venue for a Saturday night, and James appreciated that they accepted his invitation. James asked the Prophets to join him in the Tiki Lounge as the noise wasn't as bad and they could have some semblance of a conversation.

"Quite a party, bro," Kit yelled.

"Yeah, these guys like to carry on," James replied. "Follow me."

They proceeded outside to the patio where it was indeed somewhat quieter, the ambiance a stark contrast to the insanity inside. Inside, the band was playing a ZZ Top set and the attendees were getting wilder by the minute. There were already several ladies in saturated t-shirts, a precursor to the debauchery ahead. James was tired of it all. He'd seen his share of this kind of party and it was fun for a while but he now saw the emptiness of it all. The Bible says that sin is fun for a season. The problem with the DMC and millions of others was their inability or unwillingness for the party to end. James knew that partying morphed into a lifestyle and the lifestyle became abuse where a person got loaded just to be normal. The devil was patient and ruthless and there were a lot of people in that place walking around with tombstones in their eyes.

"Hey, prospect," James yelled. "Get us some more chairs!" James said as he turned and shared a laugh with the Prophets.

"Good help is hard to find," Kit said laughing.

James felt a twinge in his spirit as he barked orders to a kid who obviously didn't know what he was getting into. James had always been quite decent to prospects over the years; maybe it was his inner guilt at not ever having to endure that ritual, maybe it was that all along he was a decent guy in the wrong place. Maybe he thought too much. He knew one thing; he had more in common with the guys on the patio than any of the four hundred Doomsayers inside. That would have to be addressed at some time.

"You guys have prospects?" James asked.

"Oh, yeah," answered Kit. "We go through 'em regularly," he laughed. "Most of our prospects don't make it."

"Why's that?" James asked.

Kit looked at Tio who said, "We look at it as a humbling, not for our sake but for the sake of the prospect. You have to develop the heart of a servant and some guys aren't willing. They think they are but after six months of being the first one there and the last one to leave, most guys' pride can't handle it and they start asking when it will be over and that's when we know they'll never make it. What they don't get is that if they would hold on a little longer and never ask that stupid question, they'd make it."

"That's why we have twenty-six guys instead of a couple hundred. It's not for everyone," Kit added.

Right on cue the DMC prospect showed up with and set up enough chairs for the small group. He looked at James who said, "Not those chairs, the plastic chairs," and then laughed and told the bewildered prospect, "Just kidding bro, thanks," which made them all laugh.

Then Vonnie showed up with a platter of appetizers and a pitcher of iced tea. She was followed by another prospect with a stack of Red Solo Cups and several Cuban cigars.

James thanked her and she offered a curtsey and said, "your wish is my command," which caused every Prophet to look at James who just shrugged his shoulders and said, "I'm waiting to see what she turns into at midnight," which delighted everyone except Vonnie who good-naturedly flipped him off, spun on her heel, and walked away.

"She's gorgeous," Kit said.

"Seriously guys, I've never seen her during the daytime. I'm a little worried, nobody is that beautiful," which brought even more laughter.

"True dat," Tio said, "You know the devil won't show up wearing a red suit and a pitchfork,"

"Yeah, more like a red dress," James said to loud laughter from everyone.

The boys stuck around for some more laughs and many hugs and handshakes from what seemed like an endless procession of Doomsayers patch holders. Everyone was on their best behavior and James wondered how nice they'd be if they knew of his earlier vision. Time would tell. The men enjoyed the cigars and the conversation. James was careful to include many Doomsayers so he didn't appear aloof to his own brotherhood.

As was their custom, the Prophets started at the top and thanked Snake, Spaniard, Magic, and James for the invitation and adjourned from the party after only an hour. Kit had told James months ago that they never stuck around anywhere for long. They were all about respect and nothing about overstaying their welcome. They approached their ministry like that as well, putting enough love and scripture out there to create a curiosity, but never burying people with their preaching. It worked for them and it definitely worked for James. They ran their club like James ran his life and it had resonated with his spirit from day one at the gas station.

James knew they wouldn't stay long and he actually dreaded their departure as it would leave him alone with the DMC and with every passing hour he was more convinced that he was in the wrong place. *This is nuts*, he thought; they went all out to make my homecoming memorable and all I want to do is go back to my shop and work on a bike, alone.

James bade them a safe trip, and watched as they gathered to themselves around their six bikes and prayed together before they hit the highway. James offered a silent prayer as well, for them sure, but more for him and what lay ahead.

"Nine Ball, you doin' okay, bro?" Snake's big voice boomed behind him.

"Yeah, P, it's an awesome party. I appreciate everything," James answered.

"How's the bike running?" Snake asked.

"Incredible, bro, you guys outdid yourselves. Many thanks for that, too," he answered.

"It was the least we could do, bro; you are an example for every one of these brothers. We owed you," Snake replied.

James watched his eyes as he said, "owed" and maybe it was semantics, but James was a student of human nature and just like he didn't trust Yvonne's new-found adoration for him, he felt Snake was reminding him of the bike and the "owed" part to keep him in deference to the bigger entity, the club. It also meant that the debt was paid.

"I need to run some stuff by you; meet me out back in ten minutes, bro," Snake said.

"I'll be there, brother," James answered. *Here it comes*, he said to himself.

## Chapter Twenty-Four

Snake and his V.P., 'Spaniard,' joined James in the Tiki Lounge. You like the Tiki Lounge?" Snake laughed.

"I'm thinking of moving a pool table out here," joked James.

"You know a lot has changed since you went in; we've grown, probably more than doubled in size in the last four years, bro, and that's a good thing."

James mind was wandering to Kit's philosophy that a few committed guys was better than hundreds of "in name only" types, but he tried to focus on Snake's pitch. "We've gone from four states to seven and we've got big plans for national expansion, bro; you follow me? National. We are going to rival the biggest clubs in the world in a couple of years," he continued.

James was listening to what a few years ago would have had him bouncing off the ceiling, yet right now his mind was wandering. It was very weird. Good thing Snake couldn't read his mind or he'd have a bloody nose right now. He focused on the big man's eyes, remembering to blink occasionally to show interest. "I'm becoming the National 'P' and I'm going to nominate Spaniard as the Mother Chapter 'P' tomorrow. I figure while we have all these chapters here, we might as well have this meeting. I'll wait till after noon so the Tylenol can kick in, but we're going to have chapter meetings and then a full participation club meeting where I will make this move. You with me so far, bro?" Snake asked.

"Sure," James replied.

"Good, cause here's where you come in. I'm making a motion that you become our National Rep; you will head up all the politics of our expansion. That means travel and using your brain and your negotiating skills. It also means all the power and money you will ever need." Snake motioned for Spaniard to give them a minute alone. "Bro, do the math on four hundred guys at a hundred-bucks-a-month dues. That's now, think eight hundred, then a thousand. We are a going concern, bro. We're into a couple of businesses already. We've got bank we never had before, and with that comes power and more power and all that goes with it.

I'm offering this to you." Snake finished with a long pull from the Jack Daniels bottle he stole from the bar.

All James could think was Matthew 4:8: *Again, the devil took him to a very high mountain and showed him all the kingdoms of the world and their glory. And he said to him, All these I will give to you, if you will fall down and worship me. Then Jesus said to him, Be gone, Satan! For it is written, You shall worship the Lord your God and him only shall you serve.*

Two bikes were racing up the street and both hit fourth gear, providing a powerful backdrop to Snake's speech. At the top of fourth gear there was an explosive "THUD" and then the sound of scraping metal and screaming. James turned to Spaniard and yelled, "Call 911," and then tore through the back yard and over the cyclone fence that bordered the parking lot. Snake was right behind him as his former defensive end wheels could still move for a big man.

They ran up the embankment to the street and across the overpass to the horror at the stop sign. Both bikes had slammed into a pickup truck dragging a landscape trailer. With the bikes traveling at close to a hundred mph, the driver of the truck had no warning. He saw dark and pulled out and then saw lights; that's how these things went down.

James had been far enough from Marc and Robin that he was spared from the gore, but there was no buffer for this scene. He came upon 'Skeeter' from the El Paso chapter, who was screaming and holding the stump of his arm, which had been severed above the elbow. Both his legs were broken and folded below the knees. An arc of blood was pulsing from what was his bicep earlier. James yanked his belt from his pants and fashioned a tourniquet before scanning the street for the balance of his arm.

"Bro!" the prospect yelled. "Over there," he pointed to a leather-clad arm, complete with fingers, by the side of the road.

"Damn," James said. "Take the arm to the bar and put it in some ice," he yelled. The prospect stood in shock. James grabbed him by the shirt and shook the two hundred pound man like a rag doll. "Do you hear me? Take the arm to the bar and put it in ice!"

The prospect scrambled over and gingerly picked up the appendage and started toward the bar.

"Run!" yelled James as he ran to the bloody mess that was Tucson, a brother from Arizona who had been in the mix as long as James had. They had enjoyed many rides together over the years. Tucson was a good brother and he was dying in front of James. His side looked like hamburger meat. His denim shirt had been ground off of his body and exposed bare skin, which was full of rocks and other road excrement. Blood was pouring out of his body, from his neck to his fingers. James kneeled over his brother and fought the nausea, his eyes riveted to the ten-inch hole in Tucson's stomach. His internal organs were visible against a pulsating mass of intestine. It was horrific.

James quickly ripped off his own cut and created a pillow for his dying friend. He then tore off his t-shirt and wadded it into Tucson's stomach cavity. James could hear the sirens in the distance as he gently rocked his buddy's head in his lap. It was finally a good thing that every cop in the county knew how to get to the

Badlands in a hurry. Who says there's never a cop around when you need one?

"Tucson, it's Nine Ball, bro. I've got you, my brother, I've got you. I'm right here; Snake's right here, too. I'm not leaving you, bro; I love you, brother. Hold on, man, hold on to me. Tucson, Jesus loves you, too, bro. He took all of our sins to the cross, brother; you and I are forgiven sinners. You hear me, dog? Squeeze my hand; I need to know you're with me, bro," James begged his friend until he felt the faint but definite pressure of his friend's hand in his.

"Good, good, brother, hang in there. Listen to me, we need to deal with this right now. I love you bro, hang in here, believe with me, Jesus loves you, you understand?" Another squeeze of the hand. "Good, listen now, don't leave me! He took our sins to the cross! Listen, Tucson ... he died with our sins but he rose from the dead to give us eternal life. He's reaching out to you now. Pray with me. Lord Jesus, thank you for taking my sins. I need you. Be my savior, save my soul, live through me for eternity. I love you! Tucson! Pray this in your heart, TUCSON!" Tucson's eyes opened and James felt the strong squeeze of his brother's hand.

"I love you, Nine," his voice trailed off.

"Hold on, my brother, help is coming, I'm not leaving you. I'M NOT LEAVING YOU!" James screamed into the cold night air, his breath's hot vapor clouding the cold night sky as sobs wracked his body. A minute or two passed and James felt the giant hand of his friend and president, Snake, on his shoulder.

"Brother, you need to let these guys have Tucson."

James looked up at him with tears streaming down his face. "He's a good brother, Tucson. Me and him always rode side by side in the desert. You remember those trips to Phoenix, P? We rolled fast in that heat; we shook bottles of water at each other on the road," James said quietly.

Snake shook his head at the two CHP officers who were about to lift James off Tucson. "I'll do it," Snake said as he reached for the night's guest of honor. "Come on bro, they got him now, we gotta let them do their jobs," he said as James slowly stood.

"Kinda cold out; huh, P?" James mumbled.

Snake shook the road dirt from Nine's cut and held it like a tailor as James lifted his arms and accepted his armor. He looked like a gladiator with his muscular chest covered in blood and sweat and tears.

"Skeeter get his arm back?" James asked.

"He's on his way to the hospital; they've got the arm in a cooler," Snake replied.

"Hope they thought to take some beer with them. Skeeter likes his beer," James said.

"Let's go inside, bro, we need to get you warm and cleaned up," Snake said and then stopped his friend with his giant arm. "Hey, Nine, that was the most intensely spiritual thing I've ever seen or ever even heard of back there. It was like, I don't know, I was ... I couldn't take my eyes off of you guys. It was like I wasn't worthy of watching, but I couldn't stop."

"None of us are worthy, brother; Jesus did it all. He was with us back there. He took Tucson with him," James' voice trailed off as they both short-stepped it down the grade to the Badlands parking lot.

As they approached the front door, Vonnie was there to greet him and stopped short of hugging him seeing the blood and dirt covering his bare chest under the cut. "Oh my God, are you alright?" she asked.

"Oh, I'm fine," he laughed. "Skeeter's arm fell off and Tucson is dead, but I'm fine," he said as he walked inside. "Hey Vonnie, can you get me another shirt from my bike, doll?"

"Of course, baby, I'll be right back," she said with wide eyes.

"She'll make someone a great wife," James said to Snake.

"Just not you," Snake laughed.

"You got that right, bro," James smiled back. "Though I appreciate the gesture," he said over his shoulder. He wanted Snake to know that he knew that the club had put her up to the night's love fest and mostly that it was okay to call it off.

Chapter Last

After an Army shower and a new t-shirt, James emerged from the men's room a new man, almost. He called Snake over and asked for an audience. "It will only take a minute," he said.

Snake, still affected by the scene on the street, came to his Road Captain/National Rep and listened as James requested that he not be nominated for National Rep and furthermore, he'd like Snake's blessing as he retired from the club completely. James explained that he had an opportunity to start a church and that he was sure that he'd been called by God for this journey. He told Snake that only God could pull him from the brotherhood and that he loved and respected Snake and the other brothers for life.

Snake listened intently and respectfully before answering. "This is highly irregular, if not unprecedented; you know that. This whole conversion thing, you're definitely different and at first I chalked it up to prison, but you've been out long enough for that to fade. I don't want to lose you, bro; you know it's always been a special thing beginning back when you

313

came in the way you did. If you would have come to me an hour ago with this I would have broken your nose and taken your cut; you know that?"

James nodded, expecting the worst.

"But after what I saw up there I can't stand in your way, bro. If it's really a God thing, and I believe it is, then let's finish this charade tonight and tomorrow I will bless you out, as you call it, but you will always be my brother." Snake finished by hugging James tightly, saying, "You never know, I might come visit your church sometime."

"I'm counting on it," James said. "I'm sure everyone will understand if I roll out a bit early, all the drama and trauma and all," James said.

"I'll expect your cut tomorrow," Snake said.

"Of course. I have the utmost respect for this cut and this club, bro," James answered as he walked out the door.

Before James started his bike, he made a call to Kit, which went straight to voicemail as he was no doubt still on the highway somewhere. "Hey, bro, it's James;

gimme a call later tonight if you get a minute. I've got a question for you. Traveling mercies to you, brother. Later."

He sat on his bike for a few minutes trying to take it all in. As much as he wanted out, there was that big unknown again. *This must be the faith part*, he thought. All those people back there and only one real friend. Snake was a good man and a great leader. James prayed for him.

He turned the key, pushed start and his big bike roared to life. He pulled his 'clears' from his inside pocket, quickly fogged them up, and using his sweatshirt to ensure perfection, slid them into place. James was weird about glasses and windshields; they had to be spotless. He fastened his helmet and carefully rolled up the hill past the remaining cops and firemen and pulled over where Tucson had earlier died in his arms. "I'll see you soon, brother," James said into the night.

Then, for all the cops, for the DMC, but mainly for Tucson and his new friend Jesus Christ, he lit that bike up on the long onramp and merged onto the eastbound

Interstate at a hundred and five miles an hour and climbing. *Man, it's cold*, he thought.

## About the Author

John Andrews lives in Southern California. In addition to writing *The Outlaw Preacher*, John is the president of Promised Land Express, Inc., a refrigerated trucking company with offices in Southern California and Fort Worth, Texas. He is also president of TKO, Inc., Radically Sophisticated Christian Fashion Apparel. www.tkostore.com. John is a Charter Member and Chaplain of Prophets MC; yes, they are a real club. Check out: www.Prophetsmc.org

For comments or to schedule a speaking engagement at your church or ministry, please contact John via: www.theoutlawpreacher.com

And check out the awesome support gear!

13479358R00184

Made in the USA
Charleston, SC
13 July 2012